Khalil's Clay Creations

Diversity, Equality, and Inclusion

Eli Turner

Published by Whimsy Tales Press, 2024.

This is a work of fiction. Similarities to real people, places, or events are entirely coincidental.

KHALIL'S CLAY CREATIONS

First edition. November 20, 2024.

Copyright © 2024 Eli Turner.

ISBN: 979-8227262233

Written by Eli Turner.

Table of Contents

Preface 1
Chapter 1: Khalil's Passion for Pottery 2
Chapter 2: The Pottery Class Challenge 6
Chapter 3: A Visit to Grandma's House 11
Chapter 4: Experimenting with Patterns 15
Chapter 5: The Power of Color 20
Chapter 6: Textures and Tactile Designs 25
Chapter 7: A Field Trip to the Art Museum 29
Chapter 8: Shape Exploration: Beyond the Vase 33
Chapter 9: Learning from Friends 37
Chapter 10: Grandma's Stories of Clay 41
Chapter 11: Embracing Abstract Art 45
Chapter 12: Finding Inspiration in Nature 50
Chapter 13: Preparing for the Art Show 54
Chapter 14: Reflecting on Success and Learning from Feedback 59
Chapter 15: Khalil's Experiment with Mixed Media 63
Chapter 16: Teaching Others 68
Chapter 17: Khalil's Artistic Identity 72
Chapter 18: A Collaborative Project with the Community 77
Chapter 19: Exploring Cultural Symbolism in Art 81
Chapter 20: Experimenting with New Forms 85
Chapter 21: Khalil's Journey into Functional Art 90
Chapter 22: Embracing Environmental Sustainability in Art 94
Chapter 23: Finding Calm in Art 99
Chapter 24: Art as a Form of Healing 103
Chapter 25: Embracing Legacy and the Journey Ahead 108

Preface

Art has a special way of helping us understand the world around us and within us. *Khalil's Clay Creations* was born from the idea that everyone has something unique to offer, whether through art, words, or kindness. In this story, Khalil's journey with pottery allows him to explore not only clay and color but also themes of resilience, cultural appreciation, healing, and the joy of shared experiences. I hope this book encourages young readers to appreciate their own creativity, to celebrate differences, and to use their talents to make the world a little brighter.

Chapter 1: Khalil's Passion for Pottery

Khalil loved working with his hands. There was something almost magical in the feel of cool, wet clay between his fingers, ready to take on any shape he could dream up. To him, each lump of clay held endless possibilities, waiting to be molded, shaped, and transformed. Every time he sat down to create, his mind buzzed with ideas—vases with tall necks, round bowls with tiny patterns, little animals and figures he could set up on his windowsill, and cups with unusual twists in their designs.

At just ten years old, Khalil already spent much of his free time making things out of clay. His bedroom shelves were lined with his creations—little clay figurines of animals, a few wobbly bowls, and his favorite piece, a bumpy cup that had accidentally turned into something beautiful after a tiny crack formed. He had tried to fix it with a dab of glaze, but the imperfection made it even more special to him. He called it his "perfectly imperfect cup." His friends didn't seem to understand his fascination with pottery, but to Khalil, the process of molding clay felt like pouring out his heart. It was something personal and precious, a way he could express himself without needing words.

Khalil's family supported his creative spirit. His mother always encouraged him to bring home his creations, praising each one no matter how lopsided or rough it looked. His father, who had a gentle and kind nature, would carefully examine Khalil's pottery, turning each piece over in his hands as though it were made of gold. Khalil's grandmother, though, was his biggest fan. She had grown up in a family of artists and crafters and knew the value of handmade things. She often told Khalil that every artist had their own unique touch and that art was a gift that needed to be shared. Her words warmed Khalil's heart, giving him a sense of pride in his work even when he felt uncertain about his talent.

Yet, as much as Khalil loved working with clay, he couldn't shake a nagging insecurity. Every week, he attended a pottery class with his friends, and although he enjoyed spending time with them, he couldn't help but feel a little out of place. Many of his friends seemed to have a natural talent for creating beautiful, detailed pieces. They were quick with their hands, shaping clay into complex forms that looked impressive and polished. His friend Aminah, for example, could sculpt delicate flowers that seemed almost alive, while Musa created smooth, symmetrical bowls that always looked perfect. Khalil's own work was different—more abstract, with rough edges and unusual shapes. Sometimes, he felt that his creations looked messy compared to those of his friends, and he began to worry that he wasn't as skilled as they were.

One afternoon, his pottery teacher, Mr. Simmons, gathered the students together for an exciting announcement. Standing at the front of the class, Mr. Simmons' eyes sparkled with enthusiasm as he explained that there would be a community art show in a few months. The show was open to artists of all ages and was meant to celebrate the creativity and talent of the local community. The pottery class had been invited to participate, and each student would have a chance to display their best work. As soon as the words left Mr. Simmons' mouth, a wave of excitement rippled through the room. Khalil could feel his classmates' enthusiasm, but inside, he felt a mixture of anticipation and dread.

That evening, Khalil could hardly stop thinking about the art show. He lay in bed, staring at the ceiling, his thoughts bouncing between excitement and anxiety. On one hand, he wanted to take part; he wanted to share his pottery with others and feel the pride of displaying his work alongside that of his friends. But then, the other voice in his head reminded him that his pottery looked different—too different. What if people didn't like his style? What if they thought his pieces looked odd or unfinished? The fear of being judged made his stomach twist with unease.

The next morning, Khalil felt even more unsure about entering the art show. As he picked at his breakfast, his mother noticed his unusually quiet mood. "What's on your mind, Khalil?" she asked, her voice gentle and understanding. He hesitated for a moment, unsure of how to put his feelings into words. Finally, he admitted his fears. "I just... I don't know if I'm good enough. My pottery doesn't look like everyone else's, and I don't know if anyone would even like it at the show."

His mother listened patiently, then smiled and said, "Khalil, art isn't about looking like everyone else. It's about expressing what's inside you. Besides, you never know who might see your work and think it's wonderful. Give it a chance." Her words helped, but Khalil still felt a little nervous.

That weekend, Khalil visited his grandmother, hoping that her stories and encouragement would help ease his mind. She always had a way of making him feel better, of helping him see things from a different perspective. As soon as he entered her cozy living room, he felt the warmth and comfort of her presence. She greeted him with a big hug and led him to her collection of pottery and handmade art that decorated her home. There were pieces of all shapes and sizes—some smooth and glossy, others rough and earthy. Each piece seemed to have its own character, its own personality.

"Do you see these, Khalil?" she asked, gesturing to a beautiful but uneven vase with swirling patterns. "This was made by an old friend of mine. He always said that a piece doesn't have to be perfect to be beautiful. It just has to be true to the artist." She paused, letting her words sink in. "You know, each artist has a voice, a style that's unique to them. And that's what makes their work special. Your pottery should reflect who you are, not who you think you should be."

Khalil absorbed her words, feeling a spark of inspiration. He realized that maybe his style was different, but that didn't mean it was less valuable. Maybe, just maybe, his creations were beautiful in their own way. Spending the afternoon with his grandmother, he found himself filled with a renewed sense of purpose. They spent hours together as she shared stories of her own creative journey, how she had faced similar doubts, and how she had learned to love her style. Hearing her stories reminded him that every artist goes through moments of self-doubt, but it's pushing through those moments that allows them to grow.

Chapter 2: The Pottery Class Challenge

Khalil walked into the pottery classroom with his usual mixture of excitement and nervousness. The room was warm and smelled faintly of clay and paint, with all the pottery wheels lined up neatly along one wall and the shelves stacked high with students' projects. It was a space that always made him feel at home. The sounds of clay being slapped onto wheels, soft laughter, and the quiet whir of spinning pottery wheels greeted him as he took his place among his friends.

Today was no ordinary day, though. Khalil could feel a buzz in the air, a sense of anticipation that was different from their usual classes. His teacher, Mr. Simmons, had a mischievous smile on his face as he waited for the class to settle down. Mr. Simmons was the kind of teacher who had an energy that drew people in, a love for art that made everyone want to try a little harder and push a little further in their creative journeys. Khalil admired him and, like many of the other students, he wanted to do his best to make Mr. Simmons proud.

When the class had quieted down, Mr. Simmons began to speak, his voice filled with a lively excitement. "Alright, everyone! I have some wonderful news to share. There's going to be a community art show this spring, and guess what? Our class has been invited to take part!" He paused, letting the announcement sink in, his eyes scanning the room to gauge their reactions. As he had hoped, the class broke into excited chatter, the students turning to each other with wide eyes and eager smiles.

Khalil felt his heart skip a beat. The art show. The very thing he had been both dreaming about and dreading ever since he'd heard about it from his grandmother. He had imagined what it would be like to stand in front of his pottery pieces, surrounded by the community, but now that the chance was real, his stomach twisted into a knot of nerves. Could he really do this? Could he display his work alongside his classmates' creations and be proud of it?

Mr. Simmons continued, "Each of you will have the opportunity to choose a few pieces to display. The art show is a big deal for our community, so this is your chance to show everyone what makes your art special. You'll have a few months to work on your pieces, and I encourage you to experiment, to try things you haven't tried before, and to be bold. Remember, art is about expression. It's about telling your story through the clay."

The word "bold" echoed in Khalil's mind as he listened. He wanted to be bold, to create something that captured his thoughts, feelings, and imagination. But that nagging voice in his head reminded him of the other students. His friends—Aminah, Musa, and some of the older kids—already had such defined styles. Aminah was known for her delicate, detailed flower sculptures that seemed to blossom from the clay. Musa had a knack for creating these smooth, perfectly symmetrical bowls and cups that looked as if they'd been made by a professional. Even the younger kids, like Salma, had pieces that were admired for their bright, colorful glazes and playful designs.

Khalil's mind flashed back to his own pottery, the way his pieces seemed rough and unusual compared to his friends'. He liked his own work, yes, but he couldn't shake the feeling that others might find it strange or unfinished. He imagined people at the art show walking by, glancing at his pottery, and then moving on quickly, unimpressed. The thought made his cheeks flush, and he shifted uncomfortably in his seat.

Mr. Simmons noticed Khalil's quiet reaction and, sensing his anxiety, walked over to where he sat. "Khalil," he said, his voice soft and encouraging, "you have a real gift. Don't worry about what anyone else is doing. Focus on what you love about pottery, and let that guide you. I've seen your work, and I know it has something special. Give it a chance to shine."

Khalil looked up at his teacher, a small smile tugging at his lips despite his nerves. Mr. Simmons' words settled in his mind, and for a moment, he felt a flicker of confidence. He remembered his grandmother's advice, too, about letting his art reflect his true self. Maybe he didn't have to create the same kind of pieces as Aminah or Musa. Maybe, just maybe, he could make something that was uniquely his own, even if it didn't fit the mold.

With a renewed determination, Khalil turned his attention back to the wheel in front of him. He decided to start small, to try creating a new type of bowl that felt right to him. He remembered his favorite "perfectly imperfect cup" back home, with its unexpected crack and rough surface that somehow made it beautiful in his eyes. Inspired by that piece, he pressed his hands into the clay, shaping it into a bowl that wasn't entirely round but had a slight, intentional curve on one side. It reminded him of a wave in the ocean, rising and falling.

The more he worked, the more he found himself getting lost in the process. His hands seemed to know what to do, guiding the clay as he smoothed some parts and left others rough. He carved small lines along the side, giving the bowl an earthy texture, like the bark of an old tree. It didn't look anything like the smooth, polished bowls Musa made, but Khalil felt a sense of pride as he looked at his work. It was different, and that was okay.

As he continued to create, he couldn't help but glance over at his friends, watching them work with their own styles. Aminah was focused on adding intricate petal designs to a vase, her fingers moving with precision and skill. Musa, on the other hand, was already glazing his bowl, the vibrant blue glaze catching the light and reflecting in a way that made his piece seem almost magical. Khalil admired their work, but instead of feeling intimidated, he felt a new sense of respect for each of their unique approaches.

During the break, his friends gathered around his workbench, curious about the bowl he was working on. "Wow, Khalil, that looks really cool!" Aminah exclaimed, her eyes lighting up as she examined the textured surface of his bowl. "I love how it's not perfectly round. It makes it look more... I don't know, natural?"

Musa nodded in agreement. "Yeah, it's like it has its own story. I've never seen a bowl like this before." He reached out to touch the rough lines Khalil had carved into the side, running his fingers along the texture. "It feels different, but in a good way. You should definitely show this at the art show."

Their words filled Khalil with a warm sense of encouragement. He hadn't expected them to understand or appreciate his work, but hearing their admiration made him feel seen. Maybe his style was unique, but that didn't mean it wasn't worthy of being shared. He decided then that he would keep working on pieces that felt right to him, pieces that told his story and showed the world what he saw through his own eyes.

As the weeks passed, Khalil threw himself into his work with a renewed sense of purpose. He created bowls with uneven edges, cups with unexpected twists, and small sculptures with rough textures that seemed to embody the rawness of nature. Each piece felt like a small part of him, an expression of everything he loved about working with clay. His friends continued to cheer him on, and even Mr. Simmons took notice, often stopping by his workbench to offer encouragement and praise.

By the time the art show was only a week away, Khalil had created a small collection of pottery that he was proud of. Each piece was different, yet they all carried a similar style—a sense of wildness, of natural imperfection that he had come to love. He had found his voice, his own way of creating, and for the first time, he felt excited to share it with others.

Khalil carefully selected three pieces for the art show: his wave-inspired bowl, a cup with a spiral twist in its design, and a small sculpture of a tree, its surface textured and rough. He placed them on a tray and looked at them with a mixture of pride and anticipation.

He no longer felt the overwhelming nerves he had once felt. Instead, he was filled with a quiet confidence, a belief that his work was worth sharing, even if it was different from everyone else's.

Chapter 3: A Visit to Grandma's House

Khalil eagerly swung open the creaky front door of his grandmother's house, feeling the familiar warmth of her cozy home wrap around him like a soft blanket. The house had a comforting scent of fresh bread and herbs, mixed with a hint of old books and memories that seemed to be woven into every corner. Khalil's grandmother, whom he affectionately called "Nani," had lived in this house for as long as he could remember. It was a place filled with treasures and trinkets from her own creative journey, each piece telling its own story, and every visit was like stepping into a world of wonder and inspiration.

As soon as he entered, he spotted Nani sitting by the window, surrounded by her collection of pottery, her hands wrapped around a steaming cup of tea. Her eyes sparkled with joy when she saw Khalil, and she beckoned him over with a warm smile. "There's my little artist!" she exclaimed, setting her tea aside to pull him into a big hug. Khalil felt his worries melt away as he hugged her back. Nani's hugs were magical, filled with a kind of love that made everything seem brighter and better.

Khalil pulled out his phone and excitedly showed her pictures of his recent pottery work, including the pieces he was planning to showcase at the upcoming art show. "I wanted to show you what I've been working on, Nani," he said, his voice full of pride yet tinged with a hint of nervousness. "Mr. Simmons encouraged us to experiment and create pieces that reflect our own stories, but I'm still a little nervous about showing them to everyone."

Nani's eyes twinkled with delight as she scrolled through the photos. "Oh, Khalil, these are wonderful! I can see your heart in every piece. Each one tells its own story, doesn't it?" She paused, admiring the unique textures and shapes he had created. "You know, art is a journey. Every piece you make is a little piece of yourself, and that's what makes it special."

Khalil blushed, feeling a warm glow at her praise. "Thanks, Nani. I think I'm starting to understand what you mean. I used to think my pieces were too different, maybe even too weird, but now I'm starting to see that being different can be a good thing."

Nani chuckled softly. "Absolutely. But why don't I show you something that might help you understand a bit more?" She led him to the shelves that held her own pottery collection, each piece carefully placed as though it were an artifact in a museum. Khalil had seen these pieces many times before, but he always felt like he was seeing something new whenever he looked at them. Each one seemed to hold secrets, with textures and colors that hinted at stories from long ago.

"See this vase here?" Nani said, picking up a tall, thin vase with a slightly crooked neck. It was painted with swirls of blue and green, and its surface was textured with tiny, delicate imprints of leaves. "This piece was made by a friend of mine many years ago. She told me that it was inspired by the rivers and forests she grew up near. She said that every time she touched the clay, she imagined the soft rustling of leaves and the gentle flow of water."

Khalil listened, mesmerized, as he ran his fingers over the delicate leaf patterns. He could almost feel the river his grandmother spoke of, see the forest and hear the rustling of the trees in his mind. "It's amazing how a piece of clay can hold so much... memory," he murmured, feeling a newfound respect for the art in his hands.

Nani nodded thoughtfully. "Yes, that's the magic of pottery. Every artist has their own way of seeing the world, and they bring that vision into their work. It's not about making something perfect; it's about capturing a feeling, a memory, or a piece of yourself. This vase might not look like everyone else's, but to me, it's perfect because it's a part of my friend."

They continued exploring her collection, each piece more fascinating than the last. Some were smooth and glossy, while others were rough and earthy, with colors that ranged from vibrant reds and yellows to deep, calming blues. Nani told him stories of each piece, describing the artists and their inspirations, the ways they brought their own lives and experiences into their work. Khalil felt as though he were meeting each artist, as though he could sense a piece of their spirit in every curve and color.

At one point, Nani pointed to a small, cracked pot with a piece missing from one side. The pot was simple, with a plain glaze, but the crack gave it a raw beauty that Khalil couldn't quite put into words. "This one belonged to my grandmother," she said quietly, her fingers gently tracing the crack. "It broke one day, and I thought I'd have to throw it away. But my grandmother told me to keep it, to embrace the imperfection. She said that every flaw, every crack, is a part of the pot's story. Over time, I've come to see that the crack makes it even more beautiful."

Khalil looked at the pot, feeling a strange connection to its imperfection. He thought about his own pottery, with its rough edges and uneven surfaces, and he felt a flicker of pride. Maybe his work didn't have to be flawless to be meaningful. Maybe, like this pot, it was beautiful because it was a part of him, imperfections and all.

After spending hours listening to his grandmother's stories, Khalil felt a newfound appreciation for his own work. He realized that his pottery didn't need to be polished or perfect. Each piece could tell its own story, could hold its own meaning, even if it didn't look like everyone else's. He felt a sense of freedom he hadn't felt before, a confidence that encouraged him to explore his own style without fear or doubt.

As the afternoon wore on, Nani invited him to sit down for tea, and they settled at her kitchen table with steaming cups and a plate of warm pastries. The kitchen was filled with the golden light of the late afternoon, and Khalil felt at peace, as though the world outside had faded away, leaving just him and his grandmother and the stories they shared.

"Nani," he said thoughtfully, "do you think people at the art show will understand my work? I want to tell my story, but sometimes I worry that it's too different. What if they don't get it?"

His grandmother reached across the table, taking his hand in hers. "Khalil, the beauty of art is that it doesn't need to be understood in the same way by everyone. People will see your pieces, and each person will feel something different. Some might see the shapes, others might feel the textures, and some might just appreciate the colors. Your art doesn't need to be 'understood'—it just needs to be true to you."

Her words settled into his heart, bringing a calm certainty that he hadn't felt before. Khalil knew that he couldn't control how people would react to his work, but he could control how he felt about it. And as long as he was proud of what he had created, that was enough.

When it was time for him to leave, Nani hugged him tightly, pressing a small wrapped gift into his hand. "This is for you, Khalil," she whispered. "It's something that helped me when I was a young artist, and I hope it will help you too." She gave him a gentle smile and sent him on his way, leaving him curious about the gift in his hand.

Back home, Khalil carefully unwrapped the package to find a small, smooth stone, its surface engraved with delicate patterns that looked like waves. He held it in his palm, feeling its comforting weight, and noticed a small note from Nani tucked inside the wrapping.

The note read, "Remember, Khalil, you are as unique as this stone, shaped by the waves of life. Let your art be your story. Love, Nani."

Khalil clutched the stone in his hand, feeling a deep sense of gratitude for his grandmother's wisdom and love. He placed it on his shelf beside his pottery, a reminder of the lessons he had learned that day. Nani had taught him to see the world—and his art—in a new light. And as he prepared for the art show, he knew that he would carry her words with him, letting them guide him as he continued to shape his story, one piece at a time.

Chapter 4: Experimenting with Patterns

Khalil felt a surge of excitement as he entered his pottery class that morning. After his visit to his grandmother's house, he was inspired and ready to try something new. Her stories had filled him with ideas, and he couldn't wait to see how he could translate them into his own creations. He knew he wanted to work on something special, something that reflected the spirit of all those stories Nani had shared with him. He was eager to experiment, to create something uniquely his.

Mr. Simmons greeted Khalil with a warm smile as he settled in at his workbench. Khalil set his bag down, pulling out his sketchbook filled with notes and ideas he'd scribbled down over the past few days. He had drawn spirals, lines, dots, and shapes, all inspired by the textures and patterns he'd seen on the pottery pieces at his grandmother's house. His mind was buzzing with possibilities, and he felt his hands itch with the urge to start.

"Khalil," Mr. Simmons said as he approached, peering down at Khalil's sketches with interest. "Looks like you've been busy! I can see some really unique patterns here. Are you planning on trying some new designs today?"

Khalil nodded enthusiastically. "Yes! I visited my grandmother last weekend, and she showed me her collection of pottery. Each piece had its own pattern, and they all told different stories. I want to try and bring that into my work." He felt a mixture of excitement and nerves as he spoke, hoping his ideas would come across as well as they had in his head.

Mr. Simmons's face lit up with approval. "That's wonderful, Khalil. Patterns can add so much depth to a piece. They're a way of leaving your mark on the clay, of bringing your personality and your vision to life. I can't wait to see what you come up with."

Taking a deep breath, Khalil focused on the lump of clay in front of him. He began with a small, simple bowl, letting his hands shape it as naturally as possible. He wasn't concerned with perfection; he just wanted a blank canvas to experiment with patterns and designs. He remembered his grandmother's words, how she had spoken of the beauty in imperfections, and he tried to let go of his need for everything to look flawless.

As he worked, Khalil's mind drifted back to the images and stories his grandmother had shared. One story in particular stood out to him—a tale of a wise old potter who had once crafted bowls with swirling patterns, meant to represent the flow of life. Each swirl symbolized a different path, a different choice, and together they created a tapestry of journeys and connections. Inspired by this, Khalil took a wooden carving tool and began etching a spiral pattern along the rim of his bowl. He worked slowly, letting his hands guide him, imagining that each curve and line held a story of its own.

The first few spirals felt stiff and awkward, but as Khalil continued, his movements became more fluid, more natural. He fell into a rhythm, allowing the pattern to flow around the bowl in one continuous line. He watched as the spirals transformed the simple clay surface, giving it a sense of motion and life. The bowl seemed to come alive under his touch, as though it were a story unfolding with each line he carved.

When he finished the spirals, he looked at his work with a sense of satisfaction. The bowl was far from perfect, but it felt real, authentic. It was the first time he'd tried adding such an intricate pattern to a piece, and he was surprised by how much it changed the way he felt about his work. The pattern gave the bowl a personality, a story. He felt as though he were beginning to find his own voice, his own way of speaking through the clay.

Eager to try more, Khalil set the bowl aside and grabbed another piece of clay. This time, he decided to experiment with dots, inspired by the delicate, dot-filled patterns he had seen on one of his grandmother's vases. He formed the clay into a cup, its sides smooth and round, and began pressing small indentations along the surface, one dot at a time. He found himself falling into a steady rhythm, spacing each dot evenly, trying to create a sense of balance and harmony in the pattern.

With each dot, Khalil thought about his grandmother's stories and the many people who had shared their lives and experiences through their art. The dots began to feel like connections, like points on a map, each one representing a moment, a memory, a piece of someone's journey. He didn't worry about whether the pattern was perfect or symmetrical; he simply let it grow organically, allowing the design to emerge on its own. By the time he was finished, the cup was covered in a delicate, dotted pattern that felt almost like stars scattered across the night sky.

Khalil sat back, admiring his work, feeling a deep sense of satisfaction. Each pattern felt like a new discovery, a new way of expressing himself. The spirals, the dots—they weren't just designs; they were symbols, pieces of a language he was beginning to understand. He felt as though he were finding his own artistic voice, a way to communicate through his pottery that was uniquely his.

As he continued experimenting, Khalil tried new shapes and patterns with each piece. He carved lines into a plate, crisscrossing them to create a web-like pattern that reminded him of tree branches reaching across the sky. He etched triangles onto the side of a vase, each one slightly different in size and shape, creating a pattern that felt both chaotic and harmonious. With every piece, he felt himself growing more confident, more willing to take risks and explore new ideas.

By the end of the day, Khalil had created a small collection of pieces, each one bearing its own distinct pattern. He spread them out on his workbench, feeling a sense of pride and wonder as he looked at his creations. The spirals, the dots, the lines, and triangles—all of them felt like pieces of himself, reflections of his thoughts, feelings, and inspirations. He had discovered a new way of working with clay, one that felt deeply personal and meaningful.

As he packed up his tools, Mr. Simmons came over to admire Khalil's work. "These are incredible, Khalil," he said, his voice filled with genuine admiration. "You've found something special here. These patterns—they're like a language, a way of telling your story."

Khalil smiled, feeling a warmth spread through him at his teacher's words. "Thank you, Mr. Simmons. I think I finally understand what you mean about finding my voice. These patterns feel like... like pieces of me."

Mr. Simmons nodded, a proud glint in his eye. "That's exactly what they are, Khalil. Art is a reflection of who we are, and you're beginning to discover who you are as an artist. Keep exploring, keep experimenting. You have a gift, and the more you embrace it, the more you'll find your own unique path."

Khalil left class that day feeling inspired and fulfilled, his mind buzzing with ideas for new patterns and designs. He knew he still had a long way to go, but he was excited to continue his journey, to keep discovering new ways of expressing himself through his art. He felt grateful for his grandmother's stories, for Mr. Simmons' guidance, and for the support of his friends. They had helped him see the beauty in his own voice, in his own way of seeing the world.

Over the next few days, Khalil continued experimenting with patterns, bringing his sketchbook everywhere he went, filling its pages with ideas and designs. He found inspiration in the world around him—in the swirling leaves of a tree, the patterns in a cracked sidewalk, the stars that dotted the night sky. He began to see patterns everywhere, each one a reminder of the connections and stories that surrounded him.

Khalil's friends noticed the change in his work, and they gathered around his workbench to admire his new pieces. Aminah traced her fingers over the dots on one of his cups, her eyes wide with admiration.

"These are amazing, Khalil! They're so different from anything I've seen before. They feel… alive, like they're telling a story."

Chapter 5: The Power of Color

Khalil's fascination with pottery had grown immensely in recent weeks. Every time he walked into his pottery class, he felt a newfound excitement, a quiet but powerful urge to create something that felt like him. He had spent a lot of time experimenting with patterns, learning to carve spirals and dots, and was slowly finding his artistic voice. But something was still missing. His pieces, while meaningful to him, seemed to lack the spark, the vibrancy he longed for.

As he gazed at the shelf of his recent creations, Khalil noticed the sameness in the shades of gray and brown from the clay and the natural, unglazed look. Though he loved the earthy textures, he couldn't help but feel that his work looked plain, muted. He remembered some of the pottery in his grandmother's house—vases and bowls that seemed to glow with deep reds, soothing blues, and warm yellows. Those colors had brought the pieces to life, giving each one a unique mood and personality. Khalil wanted that feeling for his own work, a touch of color that would make his pottery stand out and tell stories in a new way.

The next day, Khalil decided to talk to his teacher, Mr. Simmons, about learning more about glazing and the use of color. As he approached Mr. Simmons, he felt a mix of excitement and nerves, wondering if he was ready to take this new step.

"Mr. Simmons," Khalil began, his voice laced with determination, "I think I want to start experimenting with color. I've been working a lot with patterns, but I feel like something's missing. I want my pieces to have... more life, more personality. I think color could help me with that."

Mr. Simmons listened carefully, nodding with understanding. "You're absolutely right, Khalil. Color has the power to transform a piece, to bring out emotions and give it depth. It's like giving your pottery a voice that speaks in different shades and tones. I'd be happy to show you how to work with glazes. It's an exciting process, but it does require patience."

Eagerly, Khalil followed Mr. Simmons to the back of the studio, where the shelves were lined with jars of glaze in every color imaginable. He looked at the rows of jars, feeling like he'd stepped into a treasure trove. There were earthy greens, deep blues, fiery reds, and soft yellows, each one calling to him, stirring his imagination. Mr. Simmons pulled down a few jars, explaining the basics of glazing.

"Glazes can be tricky," he said, holding up a jar of deep indigo glaze. "What you see here isn't always what you'll get after firing. Glazes change in the kiln, under high temperatures, and sometimes you won't know exactly what a color will look like until it's finished. But that's part of the magic of pottery—you never quite know what you'll end up with."

Khalil felt a thrill at the unpredictability of the process. He liked the idea of working with something that had a mind of its own, a color that could surprise him. He picked up a jar of blue glaze, imagining how it might look on one of his pieces. The thought of transforming his pottery with colors made his heart race. He selected a few shades—earthy green, a rich orange, and the blue he'd picked first. These colors reminded him of nature, of the world outside, and he felt that they would bring a new dimension to his work.

As he set to work, Khalil felt both excited and nervous. He took a small bowl he had carved with spirals and dipped his brush into the blue glaze, carefully applying it in smooth strokes, watching as the bowl transformed from a muted gray to a vibrant blue. He worked slowly, savoring each brushstroke, each layer of color he added. The glaze covered the clay in a glossy, smooth coat, and though he knew it would look different after firing, he could already see the way the color added life to the piece.

With each new piece, Khalil experimented with different combinations of colors, layering greens and oranges on his bowls and vases. He loved the way the colors played off each other, creating a sense of movement and depth. When he finished glazing a piece, he would carefully place it on the shelf, admiring the bright, wet colors and imagining how they would look once they were fired.

The days passed, and Khalil's excitement grew as he continued to experiment. Each day, he felt himself growing more confident, more daring with his use of color. He mixed shades, blended tones, and even tried adding specks of a contrasting color to create texture. He was beginning to see his pottery as more than just objects—they were expressions of mood, of emotion. The greens reminded him of calm forests, the reds of warm sunsets, and the blues of quiet rivers. His work was becoming a reflection of the colors he saw in the world, each piece carrying a bit of his soul.

When it was finally time to fire his pieces, Khalil placed them in the kiln with a mix of excitement and apprehension. The kiln was like a cocoon, a place where his pottery would be transformed, taking on a final form that he could only imagine. As the door closed, he felt a surge of hope, picturing the colors emerging, vibrant and alive, from the kiln's heat.

The next day, Khalil arrived at the studio early, unable to contain his anticipation. Mr. Simmons was waiting for him, and together, they opened the kiln. Khalil's eyes widened with wonder as he saw his pieces, each one transformed by the firing process. The blues were deeper than he had imagined, the greens richer, and the oranges had taken on a warmth that seemed to glow from within. Each piece looked alive, the colors dancing across the surface in patterns and swirls. It was more beautiful than he could have ever dreamed.

Khalil reached for his blue bowl, running his fingers over the glossy surface. The spirals he had carved were highlighted by the color, creating a sense of movement, as if the bowl were alive with energy. The other pieces were equally stunning. The green and orange glazes had blended in places, creating new shades that gave the pottery a sense of harmony, like different voices coming together in a song. Khalil felt a sense of pride and amazement, realizing that he had created something truly unique, something that was his own.

As he worked with color more, Khalil discovered the subtle power it had to evoke emotions and memories. He found himself drawn to certain colors on certain days, depending on how he felt. On days when he was calm, he used soft blues and greens, letting the colors wash over his pieces like gentle waves. When he felt excited or full of energy, he reached for the reds and oranges, creating bold, vibrant designs that seemed to pulse with life. He was learning to listen to his emotions, to let them guide his choice of colors, and he found that this made his work feel even more authentic, more connected to who he was.

Khalil's friends noticed the change in his pottery and gathered around to admire his work. Aminah, who loved bright colors, was especially taken with his orange and green vases. "These are beautiful, Khalil!" she exclaimed, her eyes wide with admiration. "The colors make them feel so alive. It's like they're telling a story."

Musa nodded, studying the blue bowl with spirals. "Yeah, the colors really make the patterns stand out. It's like each piece has its own mood, its own personality."

Their words filled Khalil with a deep sense of pride. He felt that he was beginning to find his voice not just in his patterns but in his colors, too. Each piece he created felt like a part of him, a reflection of his journey, his emotions, and his vision. He was learning to trust his instincts, to let his feelings guide him, and he was discovering a world of possibilities within each jar of glaze, each brushstroke, each layer of color.

As the weeks went by, Khalil continued to explore the world of color, pushing the boundaries of his creativity. He tried combining colors in unexpected ways, creating pieces that were bold and daring, pieces that told stories of his experiences, his dreams, his passions. He began to see color as a way of connecting with others, a language that went beyond words, reaching out to touch people's hearts and minds.

Through his journey with color, Khalil found a new level of confidence in his art. He was no longer afraid of his work being different, of standing out. Instead, he embraced it, knowing that his colors, his patterns, his shapes—all of it was a part of him, a reflection of his soul. And as he prepared for the upcoming art show, he felt a deep sense of pride, a belief in his work that he had never felt before.

The day of the art show was approaching, and Khalil was ready. He had poured his heart into his pieces, using colors and patterns to tell his story, to share his vision with the world. He knew that his work was unique, that it would stand out, and for the first time, he felt excited about that. He wasn't just creating pottery; he was creating a world of color and emotion, a world that was his own.

Chapter 6: Textures and Tactile Designs

Khalil arrived at pottery class that morning with his mind still swirling with the colors and patterns he had been experimenting with. As he took his seat, he ran his fingers over the clay at his workstation, enjoying the cool, soft texture beneath his hands. He'd been so focused on using patterns and colors to tell his story that he hadn't given much thought to the surface of the clay itself. But as he pressed his fingers into the soft material, he felt a spark of curiosity. He realized that the feel of the clay, its texture, could add something new to his pottery—something that could be felt, not just seen.

Mr. Simmons seemed to read Khalil's mind. As the class settled in, he walked to the front of the room, holding up a rough, unglazed pot. Its surface was uneven, covered in small ridges and grooves, and it looked nothing like the smooth, polished pieces they usually made. "Today," Mr. Simmons began, his voice calm but inviting, "we're going to focus on texture. Pottery is about more than just how a piece looks. It's also about how it feels. Texture can bring a piece to life, giving it character and dimension. It allows you to create something that people don't just see—they experience."

Khalil's eyes widened with excitement. He hadn't thought about using texture as part of his designs, but he could immediately see how it might open up new possibilities. He looked at his smooth clay and began to imagine what he could do with it. Maybe he could make it feel like tree bark or sand or even the roughness of a rocky path. The idea of creating something that felt different, something that people could interact with by touch, fascinated him.

Mr. Simmons guided them through different techniques for adding texture to clay. He showed them how to use their fingers to press small indentations, how to roll the clay against textured objects, and even how to carve patterns that would stand out from the surface. Khalil watched closely, his mind already brimming with ideas. He couldn't wait to try these techniques, to experiment with the tactile side of pottery.

Khalil decided to start with a simple project, a small bowl, so he could focus on the texture without worrying too much about the shape. He smoothed the bowl's edges, feeling the soft, malleable clay beneath his hands, and then gently pressed his thumb along the outer surface to create a series of small indents, evenly spaced around the bowl. As he worked, he realized that each press of his thumb added a little piece of himself to the clay. It was as if he were leaving tiny imprints, marks that would stay with the bowl even after it was fired and glazed.

Once he had completed the thumbprints, Khalil ran his fingers over the surface, feeling the slight dip of each indent. The bowl felt different, unique—like it had a personality of its own. He imagined someone picking it up, running their fingers over the tiny marks, and feeling the story behind each one. It was a small touch, but it added something special to the piece, something that made it his.

Emboldened by his success, Khalil decided to try a more complex texture on his next piece. He picked up a larger piece of clay and began shaping it into a cup. Once he had the basic form, he took a small, toothed carving tool and started scraping lightly along the cup's surface, creating a pattern of fine, parallel lines. He worked carefully, enjoying the rhythmic motion of the tool as it moved over the clay, leaving behind a trail of tiny ridges. Each stroke added depth and character, transforming the plain surface into something that felt alive, almost like the scales of a fish or the grooves of a seashell.

As he worked, Khalil's thoughts drifted to the textures he found in nature. He remembered running his fingers along the rough bark of trees, feeling the ridges and cracks that seemed to tell a story of growth and resilience. He thought about the feel of smooth pebbles in a riverbed, worn down by years of flowing water, and the scratchy surface of sandpaper his dad used in his workshop. These memories inspired him, giving him ideas for new ways to bring texture into his pottery.

Khalil decided to experiment further. He found a small piece of lace fabric in the studio's scrap bin and pressed it gently against the side of his cup, leaving a delicate, patterned imprint. When he lifted the fabric away, he was thrilled to see that it had left a beautiful, intricate texture on the clay. The lace pattern gave the cup a soft, almost ethereal look, as though it were draped in a gentle veil. He imagined someone running their fingers over the design, feeling the lace's delicate texture beneath their fingertips. It was a reminder that art could be both seen and felt, that it could create an experience for the senses.

His classmates noticed his experiments and gathered around, curious about his techniques. Aminah picked up one of his textured pieces, her eyes lighting up with admiration. "Wow, Khalil, this feels amazing! I've never thought about using fabric to add texture. It's like each piece has its own story you can feel."

Musa nodded in agreement, running his fingers over the ridges Khalil had carved into the cup. "This is really cool, Khalil. The texture makes it feel... alive, like it's more than just a cup. It has character."

Their admiration filled Khalil with pride and inspiration. He realized that he was beginning to create pottery that was truly his own, pottery that went beyond shape and color, that invited people to interact with it in a new way. His pieces weren't just objects to be looked at; they were experiences, invitations to touch and explore.

As the weeks went by, Khalil continued experimenting with textures, trying new techniques and materials. He used leaves to create imprints, pressed the clay against tree bark to mimic its rough surface, and even experimented with sand to give his pieces a grainy, earthy feel. Each new texture added something unique to his work, a layer of meaning that made each piece feel more alive, more connected to the world around him.

One day, Mr. Simmons surprised the class by taking them on a walk outside, encouraging them to find textures in nature that they could incorporate into their pottery. Khalil eagerly explored the small park near their studio, running his hands over rocks, tree trunks, and patches of grass, feeling the different textures and imagining how he could capture them in his work. He collected leaves, twigs, and small stones, each one a potential tool for adding texture to his pieces.

Back in the studio, Khalil pressed the leaves against a small slab of clay, leaving behind delicate, veined imprints that looked almost like fossilized plants. He used a small twig to scratch fine lines into the surface, creating a pattern that reminded him of roots branching out through the soil. These textures gave his work a sense of connection to the earth, to nature. It felt as though he were capturing a piece of the world in his pottery, preserving it in clay for others to experience.

Khalil's textured pieces quickly became his favorites. Each one held a part of his journey, a piece of the world as he saw it. He realized that texture added a new dimension to his art, a way of inviting others to connect with his work on a deeper level. He imagined people picking up his pieces, feeling the grooves and ridges, and sensing the thought and care he had put into each one. It was a form of communication, a way of sharing his story through touch.

Chapter 7: A Field Trip to the Art Museum

Khalil was brimming with excitement as he climbed onto the school bus with his pottery classmates. Today was the day of their field trip to the art museum, and he couldn't wait to see all the incredible pieces on display. He'd never been to an art museum before, and the idea of seeing real works of art up close made his heart race. Mr. Simmons had told them that the museum had a vast collection, including pottery from all over the world, each piece unique in its design, style, and purpose. Khalil was eager to learn from the masters, to see how artists throughout history had approached their craft.

As the bus rolled through the city, Khalil and his friends chatted excitedly about what they might see. Aminah was particularly interested in the sculptures, while Musa couldn't wait to see the intricate designs on ancient pottery. Khalil found himself imagining the different textures, patterns, and colors that might await him. He wondered if he would see pieces like his own—ones that celebrated natural imperfections and unique styles—or if the museum's collection would be filled with polished, traditional works. Either way, he was thrilled to explore, to immerse himself in the world of art.

When they arrived at the museum, the class gathered at the entrance, where a friendly museum guide greeted them. She introduced herself as Ms. Foster and told them that she would be taking them on a tour of the pottery and sculpture exhibits. Khalil could barely contain his excitement as they entered the first gallery. The room was quiet, filled with the soft hum of voices and the faint echo of footsteps on the polished floor. The walls were lined with display cases, each one holding pieces that seemed to carry a sense of history, of stories and lives long past.

Their first stop was a section filled with pottery from ancient civilizations. Khalil marveled at the craftsmanship, the intricate designs that adorned each piece. He examined a large clay jar decorated with swirling lines and symbols he couldn't quite decipher. Ms. Foster explained that the designs were meant to tell stories or represent important events in the lives of the people who made them. Khalil felt a surge of inspiration. These artists, just like him, had used clay to communicate their experiences, to leave a piece of themselves for others to discover. He imagined the ancient potters, hunched over their work, pressing patterns into the clay with tools made from bones or stones, each line carrying meaning.

Moving along, they came to a display of pottery from a more recent time period. Khalil noticed how the styles had evolved, how the shapes and designs had become more intricate, more detailed. He could see the progression of ideas, of techniques passed down and built upon over generations. He felt connected to these artists, even though they lived in different times and places. They were all part of a larger story, a lineage of creators who had shared the same passion for clay, for making something beautiful out of the earth.

As they moved deeper into the museum, Ms. Foster led them to a room dedicated to experimental pottery and sculpture. Khalil's eyes widened as he looked around, taking in the bold colors, the unusual shapes, the innovative designs that seemed to break every rule he'd ever learned. There was a large, asymmetrical vase covered in splashes of bright red and yellow, its surface rough and uneven, almost chaotic. Nearby, a sculpture that looked like twisted ribbons of clay was suspended in midair, each twist and turn telling a story of movement and energy.

Khalil felt his mind racing with ideas. He realized that there were no limits to what he could do with his art, that he could push boundaries, break conventions, and create pieces that were entirely his own. He had always thought of pottery as something traditional, something rooted in history and technique. But seeing these experimental works showed him that art could be anything he wanted it to be. It could be wild, bold, and unpredictable, a reflection of his own unique vision.

His favorite piece in the room was a small bowl with an unexpected twist—it had a rough, jagged edge on one side, as though the artist had chosen to leave it unfinished. The bowl was painted in soft, muted colors, and the jagged edge gave it a raw, honest quality that spoke to him. It reminded him of his own "perfectly imperfect" cup, the one with the crack that had turned a mistake into something beautiful. He felt a kinship with the artist, a sense that they understood each other's approach to pottery. He wondered if they, too, had struggled with insecurity about their work, if they had felt the pressure to conform but chose instead to embrace their individuality.

Khalil's friends were equally captivated by the artwork around them. Aminah was particularly drawn to a delicate sculpture of flowers, each petal crafted with painstaking detail, while Musa admired a collection of intricate bowls, each one painted with layers of vibrant color. They shared their thoughts with each other, pointing out their favorite pieces and discussing what they loved about each one. Khalil found himself inspired by his friends' perspectives, seeing the art through their eyes, appreciating details he might have overlooked on his own.

As they continued through the museum, they entered a gallery filled with pottery that incorporated elements of nature. Khalil was immediately drawn to a large, earthy-colored vase adorned with leaves, flowers, and branches. The artist had pressed real leaves into the clay before it dried, leaving delicate imprints that looked almost like fossils. Khalil ran his fingers along the surface, feeling the gentle ridges and dips where the leaves had left their mark. He thought about his own textured designs, how he had pressed leaves and other natural objects into his pieces. It made him feel connected to this artist, as though they shared a common language, a mutual respect for nature and its beauty.

The class continued their tour, moving from one exhibit to another, each one revealing new ideas, new possibilities. Khalil found himself filled with excitement and curiosity, each piece sparking a new idea, a new approach he wanted to try. By the time they reached the end of the tour, his mind was buzzing with inspiration, his sketchbook filled with quick drawings and notes on techniques he wanted to explore. He felt like he'd discovered a world of possibilities, a world where art could be anything he wanted it to be.

Chapter 8: Shape Exploration: Beyond the Vase

Khalil walked into his pottery class feeling inspired but challenged. After the museum trip, he had been filled with ideas about colors, patterns, and textures. But there was one aspect of pottery he hadn't fully explored: shape. He usually worked with classic forms—simple bowls, cups, and vases. These shapes were familiar and comfortable, but Khalil was starting to feel like he was ready to try something new, something that pushed him to rethink what pottery could be.

He took a seat at his workstation, rolling a ball of clay between his hands as he thought about all the unconventional shapes he'd seen at the museum. Some pieces had looked more like sculptures than functional objects. He had been particularly captivated by a piece shaped like a twisting spiral, its structure complex yet balanced, as though it were in constant motion. Khalil wanted to try creating something that broke away from tradition, something that wasn't just a cup or a bowl but a piece that told its own story through its shape.

Mr. Simmons walked by, noticing Khalil's thoughtful expression. "Thinking about something new, Khalil?" he asked with a warm smile. Khalil nodded, voicing his desire to step outside of his comfort zone and explore more unconventional forms.

"That's a great idea," Mr. Simmons replied encouragingly. "Sometimes the most interesting pieces come from letting go of functionality and focusing on the shape itself. Try thinking about the movement, the flow, the emotion you want the piece to convey. Let your hands lead, and see where the clay takes you."

Khalil found Mr. Simmons's words reassuring. He looked down at the ball of clay in his hands and decided to let go of any specific plan, to let the shape emerge naturally. He began by pressing his thumbs into the clay, hollowing out the center to form the base. But rather than shaping it into a traditional round or oval form, he started stretching and pulling the sides, twisting them slightly to create gentle curves. He found himself imagining a wave, a smooth, flowing movement that captured a sense of calm and strength.

As he molded the clay, Khalil noticed that he was no longer thinking about what the piece "should" look like. Instead, he was focused on how it felt, how each curve and twist seemed to bring the clay to life. The shape grew taller, slender yet winding, with a gentle spiral at the top. He hadn't started with any particular design in mind, but as the shape took form, he realized that it reminded him of the waves he loved watching by the sea on family vacations. It was a piece that felt like it was in motion, like it could almost sway with the breeze.

Khalil was so absorbed in his work that he barely noticed when his classmates gathered around to watch him. Aminah leaned over his shoulder, her eyes wide with admiration. "That's amazing, Khalil! It looks so... alive. It's like you've captured a wave in clay!"

Musa nodded in agreement, studying the piece thoughtfully. "It's really different from anything you've done before. It doesn't look like a vase or a bowl; it's just... itself. I think that's what makes it so unique."

Khalil felt a surge of pride at his friends' compliments. He realized that this was what he had been searching for—this freedom to create something that didn't have to fit into a specific category. His piece wasn't a vase or a cup; it didn't need to hold anything or serve a particular purpose. It was simply an expression, a shape that carried meaning through its form alone.

Encouraged by his success, Khalil decided to try more experimental shapes. His next project was inspired by a tree he often sat under at the park. He closed his eyes, imagining the thick, sturdy trunk, the branches reaching out in all directions, each one twisting and bending toward the sunlight. He wanted to capture that same sense of growth and strength, to create a piece that felt as rooted and alive as the tree itself.

This time, he began with a wide, solid base, pressing the clay firmly to create a foundation that felt strong and stable. He then pulled up sections of the clay, shaping them into slender, branching forms that twisted and spread, much like the limbs of a tree. He allowed each "branch" to move in its own direction, some reaching upward, others bending to the side, giving the piece an organic, almost wild appearance.

As he worked, Khalil felt a connection to the tree, to the way it grew and adapted over time. The shape of the piece reminded him that life was unpredictable, that growth often required bending and changing direction. It was a lesson he hadn't expected to learn from clay, but one that felt deeply meaningful.

By the time he finished, his piece looked more like a sculpture than anything functional. It was abstract, with twisting forms that captured a sense of life and movement. Khalil felt a deep satisfaction, a sense that he had tapped into something new within himself. He was no longer just making pottery; he was creating art, pieces that went beyond function to explore ideas, emotions, and stories.

Over the next few weeks, Khalil continued to experiment, allowing himself to play with shapes and forms he had never attempted before. He made a piece that resembled a mountain, with jagged edges and steep ridges, inspired by his family's trips to the hills. He created another piece that looked like a winding river, the clay flowing and curving in gentle waves. Each new form felt like an exploration, a journey that took him deeper into his own creativity.

Khalil's classmates noticed the change in his work, and many of them began to experiment with their own shapes, inspired by his willingness to try something different. Aminah, who usually focused on delicate flower sculptures, tried making a piece inspired by a bird in flight, its wings spread wide in mid-motion. Musa, who favored smooth, symmetrical bowls, created a bowl with a rough, uneven edge that looked like the edge of a cliff. The studio was filled with excitement and creativity, each student pushing their boundaries and discovering new ways of expressing themselves.

Mr. Simmons was thrilled with the class's enthusiasm. He encouraged them to continue exploring, to let their imaginations guide them. "Remember," he told them, "art doesn't have to be practical. Sometimes the most powerful pieces are the ones that don't serve any function, that simply exist to express an idea or feeling. Let your shapes tell a story."

Khalil took Mr. Simmons's words to heart. He started thinking of his pieces as stories, each shape capturing a moment or memory, a feeling he wanted to share. He stopped worrying about whether his work was "useful" and focused instead on creating pieces that felt meaningful to him.

One of Khalil's favorite creations was a piece inspired by a memory of sitting by a river with his grandmother. The clay twisted and turned like a flowing stream, with small, pebble-like forms he had added to represent stones along the riverbed. It wasn't a piece he could use to drink from or display flowers, but it was one that made him feel connected to that moment, to the warmth and comfort of being with his grandmother by the water. The piece was a reflection of that memory, a way for him to capture it in a form that he could hold in his hands.

As he looked at his collection of experimental shapes, Khalil felt a sense of pride and fulfillment he hadn't felt before. Each piece was unique, a reflection of his journey, his willingness to explore and push beyond the familiar. He realized that he had discovered a new side of himself as an artist, one that valued expression over function, creativity over convention.

Chapter 9: Learning from Friends

Khalil loved the growing energy and excitement in the pottery studio. After weeks of experimenting with color, texture, and shape, he had grown tremendously as an artist. His pottery now reflected his unique voice, and he felt more confident in his creations. But what thrilled him the most was how his entire class had embraced this journey of exploration alongside him. The pottery studio, once filled with predictable shapes and classic designs, was now a vibrant mix of colors, patterns, and forms, each piece reflecting the imagination and personality of his friends.

One afternoon, Khalil arrived early to find Aminah already at her workstation, her hands gently pressing a soft, pastel-colored clay into a delicate flower shape. She was known for her talent in crafting realistic-looking flowers, each petal beautifully sculpted with precision. Today, she was working on a small rosebud, the petals curling just slightly to give the impression that the flower was about to bloom. Khalil watched in quiet admiration, noticing how careful and gentle her movements were, each touch deliberate and thoughtful.

"Wow, Aminah, that's beautiful," he said, leaning closer to get a better look. "I don't know how you make the petals look so real. They almost look like they'd be soft to the touch, like an actual flower."

Aminah smiled, her eyes lighting up with pride. "Thank you, Khalil. I've been practicing this for a while now. It's all about layering the clay thinly, working from the center out, and shaping each petal individually. You have to imagine the flower growing, how each petal unfolds. That's what gives it that soft, delicate look."

Khalil listened carefully, fascinated by her approach. He realized that while he had focused on experimenting with bold, abstract shapes, Aminah had mastered the art of subtlety and detail. Her work required patience, a skill he sometimes struggled with. Watching her work, Khalil thought about his own techniques and wondered if he could incorporate some of her methods into his pieces. He wanted to try creating a sense of gentleness and realism, something he hadn't focused on before.

He decided to spend the afternoon practicing, attempting to sculpt something more intricate than his usual abstract forms. Inspired by Aminah's roses, he began molding a small leaf, trying to capture its delicate lines and the fine veins that ran across its surface. It was more challenging than he'd anticipated. He kept getting frustrated as the veins blurred or the edges turned too thick. But as he focused, channeling the patience and care he had seen in Aminah's work, he started to see progress. The leaf took shape, its edges smooth and its veins lightly etched, delicate yet defined.

Aminah noticed his efforts and walked over to offer tips, showing him how to hold the tool gently, how to adjust the pressure for different details. With her guidance, Khalil managed to finish his leaf, a piece that carried a new sense of intricacy and realism he hadn't achieved before. It felt like a small victory, and he was grateful to Aminah for her help.

The next day, Khalil watched Musa at his workstation, studying the way he approached glazing. Musa had always been the best with color, his pieces glowing with bright, bold shades that seemed to lift right off the clay. Today, he was working on a series of small bowls, each one glazed in a gradient that shifted from deep blue to vibrant turquoise. Khalil was amazed at the smooth transition between colors, the way the shades blended seamlessly, creating an effect that reminded him of the ocean waves.

"How do you get the colors to blend like that?" Khalil asked, genuinely curious.

Musa grinned, clearly pleased to share his technique. "It's all about layering," he explained, holding up one of the bowls. "I start with a base coat and let it dry completely. Then, I layer the second color on top, overlapping the edges slightly. You have to move the brush in light, circular motions, almost like you're painting with air. That way, the colors merge without any harsh lines."

Khalil watched Musa demonstrate the technique, his brush moving in slow, steady circles. The glaze settled in soft waves, the colors melting into one another beautifully. Khalil realized that this technique required a steady hand and an eye for subtlety, skills he hadn't thought about when using bolder colors. He decided to give it a try, selecting two shades—an earthy green and a soft brown—that reminded him of a forest in late autumn.

Following Musa's instructions, he layered the colors carefully, adjusting his brushstrokes to create a gradual, natural transition. At first, it felt awkward; his hand shook slightly, and the colors didn't blend as smoothly as he'd hoped. But with Musa's encouragement, he kept at it, slowly finding his rhythm. By the time he finished, his bowl had a gentle, earthy gradient, a blend of colors that felt calming and organic. Khalil was thrilled with the result, feeling as though he had unlocked a new aspect of his creativity.

In the weeks that followed, Khalil continued learning from his friends, absorbing their techniques and incorporating them into his own style. Each friend had a unique approach, a particular strength, and Khalil found himself inspired by their perspectives. He admired how each artist saw the world differently, how their personalities shone through their work. It made him appreciate the diversity of their talents, the richness that came from combining their ideas and techniques.

One day, Mr. Simmons encouraged them to work on a group project, a collaborative piece that would represent the class as a whole. The idea was for each student to contribute their own section, using their preferred techniques and styles, and then combine the sections into one large, cohesive piece. Khalil was excited by the idea; it was a chance to blend all the skills they had learned from each other, to create something that celebrated their individuality and unity.

The class decided on a large, circular mural made of interconnected tiles. Each tile would represent a different aspect of nature—flowers, trees, rivers, and mountains—and the final piece would be a celebration of the natural world. Aminah took charge of the floral tiles, sculpting delicate petals and vines in her signature style. Khalil, inspired by his recent experiments with shape and texture, worked on the mountain tiles, crafting rugged, jagged forms that conveyed strength and resilience. Musa focused on the rivers, using his glazing skills to create tiles with gradients of blue and green that mimicked the flow of water.

As they worked, Khalil found himself learning even more. Watching Aminah, he gained a new appreciation for detail, for the way tiny, subtle touches could transform a piece. He saw how Musa's mastery of color brought life to the rivers, how his brushstrokes created a sense of movement and depth. And through his own work, Khalil found a new level of confidence, a belief in his ability to contribute meaningfully to the mural. Each tile was a reflection of its creator, and together, they formed a story of friendship, growth, and shared inspiration.

When the mural was finally complete, the class gathered to admire their work. The circular pattern of the tiles created a beautiful sense of unity, each section flowing seamlessly into the next. Aminah's flowers led into Khalil's mountains, which blended into Musa's rivers, creating a continuous narrative that captured their journey as a class. The mural was more than just a piece of art; it was a testament to the power of collaboration, to the way they had all grown and learned from each other.

Chapter 10: Grandma's Stories of Clay

On a quiet Saturday morning, Khalil found himself once again at his grandmother's cozy house, an old brick home nestled among tall, swaying trees. The sun cast soft, warm light across the living room, illuminating her collection of pottery pieces that lined the shelves, each one as unique and full of life as she was. His grandmother, or Nani, as he affectionately called her, had invited him over with a special purpose in mind. She had promised to share more of her stories about the pottery pieces in her collection, stories she said held secrets of art and life, passed down from artists who, like Khalil, had poured their dreams and experiences into the clay.

Khalil settled comfortably into the large armchair beside her, glancing around the room with a sense of excitement. Every shelf and tabletop was filled with handcrafted items—some were elegant and polished, others rough and earthy, but each had its own story, as if every piece whispered memories of the hands that had shaped it. His grandmother's warm smile and inviting eyes made him feel as though he were about to embark on a journey through time.

As they began, Nani carefully picked up a small, round pot with a soft, sandy texture, its surface dotted with faint, uneven lines. She held it reverently, tracing her fingers over the marks. "This one," she began, her voice gentle, "was made by an old friend of mine, a potter who believed that art should feel like the earth itself—imperfect, textured, and alive." She paused, her eyes twinkling as she turned the pot in her hands. "He once told me that he left the marks from his tools on the surface as a way of honoring the journey, the process. Every scratch and line tells the story of how the clay was transformed, how it went from a rough lump to a finished piece."

Khalil listened closely, feeling the weight of her words. The pot was simple, even humble, but knowing that it represented the journey of creation made it seem so much more meaningful. He thought of his own work, the times he'd worried about smoothing out every line, erasing every trace of the process. He realized now that those marks—the little reminders of the journey—gave his work its own story, its own life. His grandmother's friend had embraced those imperfections as a testament to the act of creation itself.

Next, Nani picked up a tall, slender vase with a glossy, dark green glaze. The vase was adorned with intricate patterns of leaves and vines that curled around its surface, as if the plants were growing and reaching toward the light. "This vase," she said, "was crafted by a young potter who had a deep love for nature. She spent hours studying the plants and trees around her, and she believed that each leaf, each flower, was a piece of art. She didn't want her pottery to be just objects; she wanted them to reflect the beauty of the natural world, to remind people of the earth's gifts."

Khalil looked at the vase with a newfound appreciation, noting the delicacy of the vines and the way they seemed to flow naturally over the clay. He thought about how he, too, had been inspired by nature—the leaves he'd pressed into his own clay, the rough textures he'd created to mimic tree bark. The vase was more than just an object; it was a tribute to the world outside, a reminder that art could be a celebration of the beauty around us.

They continued through her collection, and each piece seemed to hold a deeper, richer story. There was a heavy, dark bowl with a thick, jagged rim, its surface unglazed and rough to the touch. Nani explained that it had been made by a potter who embraced strength and resilience, who saw beauty in raw, unpolished surfaces. "He believed that the clay should speak for itself," she said, her voice filled with admiration. "He didn't want to hide its natural texture or cover it with glazes. To him, this rough surface was a reminder of the earth's strength, its ability to withstand storms and grow anew. He wanted people to feel the rawness of the clay, to be reminded of their own strength."

Khalil ran his fingers over the bowl's rugged surface, feeling the uneven texture beneath his skin. He could imagine the artist's hands shaping it, his choice to leave it unglazed a bold declaration that beauty didn't have to be smooth or polished. Khalil thought about his own journey, the times he'd struggled with doubts, the moments when he'd felt uncertain about his work. This bowl, with its strength and resilience, reminded him that art, like life, was often about embracing challenges, about finding beauty in the raw and unrefined.

One of the most fascinating pieces was a wide, shallow dish with an intricate pattern of spirals carved into its surface. The spirals seemed to flow and interconnect, creating a mesmerizing effect that drew Khalil's eyes across the dish in continuous, unending paths. Nani told him that this dish was made by an artist who believed that life was a journey, filled with twists and turns. "He once told me that each spiral represents a choice, a path we take," she explained, her fingers tracing the pattern. "Together, they form a web of experiences, a reminder that our lives are shaped by the paths we choose."

Khalil felt a sense of awe as he looked at the dish, imagining the artist's philosophy of life woven into the pattern. It made him think about his own choices, the decisions he'd made to pursue pottery, to explore new techniques and styles, to embrace his individuality. Each choice, each path, had led him to where he was now, had shaped him into the artist he was becoming. The spirals were a reminder that art could capture the complexity of life, the interconnected moments and choices that made each person's journey unique.

The day wore on, and Khalil found himself lost in Nani's stories, each one a window into the lives and thoughts of artists who had poured their souls into their work. He felt as though he were walking in their footsteps, learning from their experiences and insights. Nani's voice was soft yet vibrant, filled with a reverence for the artists and their creations. Each piece she shared with him became a lesson, a reminder that art was more than just an object; it was a piece of the artist's heart, a reflection of their passions, struggles, and dreams.

As the afternoon light began to fade, Nani picked up one final piece—a small, unassuming cup with a delicate crack running along its side. Khalil recognized it immediately; it was the "perfectly imperfect" cup he had admired so many times before, the one he had drawn inspiration from when he'd first begun exploring his own style. Nani smiled as she held it out to him, her eyes filled with a gentle wisdom.

"This cup," she said, "was made by a potter who understood that life, like clay, doesn't always go as planned. She was shaping this cup when a small crack formed, and at first, she was disappointed, thinking it had ruined the piece. But then, she decided to embrace the imperfection, to see it as a part of the cup's story. She kept it, a reminder that sometimes beauty comes from the unexpected, from the flaws and imperfections that make each piece unique."

Khalil held the cup in his hands, feeling the crack beneath his fingers. It was a simple piece, yet it carried a profound lesson. He thought about his own struggles with perfection, his fears of making mistakes, and the times he'd been tempted to give up when things didn't go as planned. The cup reminded him that art, like life, was a journey filled with surprises, that every flaw, every unexpected twist, was an opportunity to grow, to learn, and to create something beautiful.

Chapter 11: Embracing Abstract Art

Khalil's pottery journey had been full of growth and discovery, and by now he felt a deep connection to his work. Each piece he crafted reflected something about himself, and he found satisfaction in creating pottery that told stories and captured moments. But there was a part of him that longed to go even further, to create pieces that weren't confined by tradition, functionality, or even recognizable forms. He wanted to explore the abstract, to push the boundaries of what pottery could be. This desire had grown ever since his trip to the art museum, where he'd seen pieces that defied convention, pieces that weren't cups or bowls or vases but raw, expressive forms that seemed to speak directly to the heart.

One afternoon, Khalil sat at his workbench, a lump of clay in front of him and an open mind. He decided that today, he wouldn't create anything familiar; he would let his hands guide him, responding to the clay's shape and feel rather than focusing on any particular goal. He closed his eyes for a moment, letting go of any expectations, allowing himself to feel the clay without overthinking it. Slowly, he began to mold it, pushing and pulling, twisting and shaping. The piece began to take form, though it didn't resemble anything specific—it was neither symmetrical nor smooth. It was, instead, unpredictable, almost chaotic, with ridges, curves, and folds that seemed to spring up naturally from his movements.

He let himself get lost in the process, feeling a strange freedom in creating something undefined. Without the constraints of function or tradition, he felt as if he were discovering something about himself with each press of his fingers, each twist of the clay. The piece began to look like a wave, its ridged surface flowing in a spiral that almost felt alive, as if it held an untamed energy, a sense of movement that couldn't be pinned down. He added subtle lines with his carving tool, not in any specific pattern but as an echo of the flow he saw within the shape.

When he finally set his hands down, he stared at the piece, feeling a mixture of awe and excitement. It didn't look like anything he had made before. It was abstract, without a clear beginning or end, and yet it felt whole, complete in its own way. He realized that he had created something that spoke to him on a personal level, something that expressed a feeling rather than a function.

Aminah, who had been working nearby, noticed his new piece and came over to take a closer look. Her eyes widened as she studied it, tracing the twists and curves with her gaze. "Khalil, this is incredible," she said, her voice filled with admiration. "It's like... I don't know how to describe it. It looks alive, like it has its own story. It makes me feel something, even though it doesn't look like anything specific."

Her words struck a chord with Khalil. He realized that abstract art had the power to evoke emotions without the need for clear shapes or forms. His piece didn't have to "be" anything; it simply had to exist, to capture a feeling that others could connect to in their own way. The thought excited him, giving him a sense of creative freedom he hadn't felt before. He decided to continue exploring this style, to see where his hands—and his heart—would lead him.

Over the next few weeks, Khalil threw himself into abstract pottery with enthusiasm. He experimented with different shapes, creating pieces that twisted, stretched, and folded in unexpected ways. He stopped worrying about symmetry and balance, allowing each piece to develop naturally, following the flow of his hands and instincts. He made a piece with sharp, jagged edges, capturing a sense of tension and strength, and another with gentle, curving lines that seemed to soothe and calm the eye. Each piece felt like an expression of his mood, his thoughts, a way of communicating emotions that words couldn't capture.

One day, he decided to create a piece inspired by the feeling of joy—a pure, unfiltered happiness that made him want to laugh out loud. He thought about what joy looked like, how it moved and felt.

He began shaping the clay with quick, light movements, allowing it to take on a lively, almost bouncy shape with curves that seemed to dance. As he worked, he added small, circular indentations along the sides, as if the clay itself were bubbling over with laughter. The finished piece looked almost whimsical, its shape a celebration of joy in its purest form. Khalil felt a deep sense of satisfaction, a belief that he had captured something real and alive.

In contrast, another day, Khalil found himself feeling introspective, lost in thought as he sat at his workbench. He decided to create a piece that reflected this quieter, more contemplative mood. His movements were slower, more deliberate, and the shape that emerged was dark and grounded, with thick lines that wrapped around it like layers of thought. The piece looked heavy, almost solemn, with a weight that seemed to hold secrets, memories, and reflections. He realized that, through abstraction, he was able to capture a side of himself he hadn't expressed before, a depth that he felt but hadn't been able to articulate.

His friends noticed the shift in his work and often gathered around to see what he had created. Each piece sparked a different reaction, and Khalil loved hearing their interpretations, their personal connections to his work. Aminah once described one of his pieces as "a storm frozen in time," while Musa called another "the shape of a daydream." Khalil was fascinated by how each person saw something different in his pieces, how abstract art allowed them to see their own emotions and experiences reflected in his work. He felt as though he were creating a mirror, a way for people to see themselves through his art.

As he continued down this path, Khalil's understanding of art began to change. He no longer felt the need to control every detail, to shape each piece into something recognizable. Instead, he embraced the unknown, the freedom to create without a plan, without expectations. He began to see beauty in spontaneity, in the way clay could take on a life of its own, revealing shapes and forms that surprised even him. Each piece was a journey, a discovery that unfolded in his hands, and he relished the thrill of not knowing where it would lead.

Mr. Simmons noticed Khalil's shift toward abstraction and encouraged him to keep exploring, to push the boundaries even further. One day, Mr. Simmons gathered the class and introduced them to the idea of "intuitive art"—a form of creation guided by emotion, by instinct rather than by thought. He challenged them to create a piece without planning, without sketches or preparation, to simply let their feelings guide their hands. The idea excited Khalil, and he eagerly accepted the challenge.

He sat down with a lump of clay, closing his eyes for a moment to clear his mind. He took a deep breath and let his hands move, shaping and molding without thinking. His fingers pressed into the clay, creating curves and indentations, a shape that began to unfold like a story. He felt a wave of emotions rise within him—hope, excitement, even a hint of vulnerability. When he opened his eyes, he saw a form he hadn't expected, a piece that looked like a twisting vine reaching upward, as if reaching for light. The shape was raw, imperfect, but it held a truth that resonated with him.

As he continued to work on it, Khalil realized that he was pouring a part of himself into the piece, letting it capture his hopes, his dreams, his desire to grow and find his own path. He added texture to the surface, roughening some areas while leaving others smooth, creating a contrast that reflected his journey. It was a piece unlike anything he had made before, a reflection of his inner world, his feelings laid bare in clay.

The experience changed something within Khalil. He realized that art could be a mirror, a way of seeing himself more clearly, of understanding his own heart. He no longer felt bound by rules or expectations; he was free to create as he wished, to let his art be a reflection of his soul. He felt a sense of liberation, a belief that he was on a path uniquely his own, guided by his instincts, his emotions.

Each new piece he created felt like a step forward, a journey deeper into himself. He experimented with bold shapes, unexpected textures, even combining colors in ways that felt daring and new. He found that, through abstraction, he was able to capture emotions he hadn't known how to express. His pieces became a language, a way of communicating without words, and he loved the feeling of freedom, of discovering new parts of himself with each creation.

When he shared his abstract pieces with his friends and family, Khalil was touched by their responses. His grandmother looked at one piece and described it as "a dance between light and shadow," while Mr. Simmons called another "a glimpse into the soul." Each person saw something different, and Khalil loved hearing their interpretations, their connections to his work. He realized that abstract art allowed people to see themselves, to find their own meanings, their own stories.

Chapter 12: Finding Inspiration in Nature

One crisp Saturday morning, Khalil woke up with an urge to get outside and find inspiration in the world around him. He had spent so many hours working with clay indoors that he felt a need to reconnect with nature, to draw inspiration from the textures, shapes, and colors that existed in the natural world. The previous months had been a journey of growth, from learning about color and pattern to exploring texture and shape, and finally, to discovering the freedom of abstract expression. But Khalil felt there was something more, a deeper layer he hadn't yet tapped into. His teacher, Mr. Simmons, had once mentioned that many artists find their most powerful inspiration outdoors, where the unpredictability of nature could spark creativity in surprising ways. Khalil was ready to see if that would be true for him as well.

He packed a small backpack with his sketchbook, pencils, and some snacks, and headed to a nearby park that was known for its winding trails, dense groves of trees, and sparkling river. As he entered the park, he was greeted by the gentle rustling of leaves and the crisp scent of pine in the air. Khalil walked slowly, taking in his surroundings, allowing his mind to relax and become open to whatever inspiration he might find.

The first thing that caught his attention was a cluster of rocks near the entrance of the trail. Each rock was unique, with its own color, shape, and texture. Some were smooth and rounded, others rough and jagged. Khalil knelt down, running his fingers over their surfaces, feeling the coolness and the contrast between them. He was struck by how each rock seemed to tell its own story, shaped by time, weather, and its journey through the elements. In his mind, he imagined creating pottery that captured these qualities—pieces that felt ancient, timeless, with textures that reflected the resilience of these rocks.

He took out his sketchbook and began to draw, letting the shapes of the rocks guide his hand. He experimented with lines and shading, trying to capture the rough edges, the shadows, and the smooth curves. As he drew, he began to see how he could translate these forms into his pottery, using different textures and glazes to mimic the look and feel of stone. The idea excited him, and he filled several pages with sketches, each one capturing a different aspect of the rocks he saw before him.

After a while, he continued down the trail, listening to the soft crunch of leaves underfoot and the distant chirping of birds. The trees around him were tall and majestic, their trunks thick and their branches stretching high above, forming a canopy that filtered the sunlight into dappled patterns on the ground. Khalil felt a sense of awe and humility as he looked up at the towering trees. They were like silent giants, witnesses to countless seasons and changes, standing strong through time. He imagined capturing that sense of endurance, of growth, in his own work.

He stopped at the base of a particularly old tree, its bark thick and ridged, with deep grooves that looked like ancient carvings. He ran his fingers over the bark, feeling the roughness and the uneven texture. He thought about how he could create a similar texture on his pottery, maybe by pressing different materials into the clay to create those natural ridges and patterns. He was beginning to see how his art could reflect not just what he saw but what he felt in these moments—how the rough bark made him feel grounded and connected to something much larger than himself.

Khalil decided to sit by the tree for a while, sketching its shape, the twisting branches, the leaves that fluttered in the breeze. He imagined a piece of pottery that captured the essence of the tree, with a tall, sturdy base and branches that extended outward, perhaps as handles or decorative lines etched into the surface. He let his mind wander, allowing ideas to flow freely, feeling a connection between himself and the natural world that filled him with inspiration.

As he continued walking, he came to a clearing where a small, sparkling stream meandered through the trees, its water clear and cold as it tumbled over rocks and fallen branches. The stream seemed alive, constantly moving, constantly changing, yet always flowing in a single direction. Khalil felt mesmerized by its rhythm, the way the water caught the sunlight and reflected it in tiny sparkles. He imagined capturing that movement, that sense of flow, in a piece of pottery, creating a form that seemed to spiral or twist, like water flowing in a river.

He took out his sketchbook again, drawing the lines of the stream, the rocks that interrupted its flow, and the small eddies that formed around them. He thought about how he could use glazes to mimic the look of water, layering blues and greens to create depth, and adding a glossy finish to give it a sense of wetness. He realized that nature didn't just offer shapes and textures but also motion and energy. His pottery could reflect these qualities, becoming more dynamic, more alive.

As he sat by the stream, he felt a deep sense of peace, as though he were a part of the world around him. He listened to the soft trickling of water, the whisper of the wind through the leaves, and the occasional call of a bird. It reminded him that art didn't have to be separate from nature; it could be an extension of it, a way of capturing the essence of the world around him. He felt a sense of gratitude for the beauty that surrounded him, for the inspiration it gave him, and he resolved to bring this feeling back into his pottery.

After a while, he continued on, climbing a small hill that overlooked the park. From the top, he could see the landscape stretched out before him—the trees, the river, the rocks, and the distant mountains on the horizon. The view filled him with a sense of wonder and possibility, reminding him of how vast and beautiful the world was. He felt a surge of creativity, as though he could capture the entire landscape in a single piece of pottery, each part of nature contributing to a greater whole.

He began sketching again, this time trying to capture the shapes of the hills, the lines of the river, and the outline of the distant mountains. He thought about how he could create pottery that reflected the land itself, using earthy colors and natural shapes, incorporating textures that felt as ancient and enduring as the rocks and trees around him. He felt a connection to the land, a desire to honor it in his work, to create pieces that spoke of the beauty and resilience of nature.

Chapter 13: Preparing for the Art Show

With the art show only a few weeks away, Khalil found himself both excited and nervous. The studio was buzzing with energy as his classmates prepared their final pieces for display. Each student had been given a small section of the exhibit space to showcase their work, a chance to share their individual journeys with the community. Khalil felt honored to have his own display, but he also felt the weight of responsibility that came with it. This was his opportunity to show the world what he had learned, what he had discovered through his art, and he wanted his pieces to capture the growth, inspiration, and emotions he'd experienced.

Khalil had created many pieces over the past months, each one reflecting a different part of his journey. There were the abstract shapes that told stories of freedom and expression, textured bowls that captured the essence of nature, and pieces with intricate patterns inspired by his grandmother's collection. He felt proud of each one, but he knew he couldn't display everything. He needed to choose a selection that would represent his journey in a way that was honest and meaningful.

He decided to take his time with the selection process, setting aside entire afternoons to sit with his pieces, studying each one, letting the memories of creating them wash over him. Some of the pieces were immediately clear choices—like the "perfectly imperfect" cup he had first crafted and the abstract wave that embodied his exploration of shape and motion. These pieces were milestones, markers of his growth as an artist, and he knew they had to be part of his display.

However, as he went through his work, he encountered pieces that he felt unsure about, pieces that had been challenging or didn't turn out exactly as he had envisioned. He wondered if these should be included, too, as reminders of his learning process. After some thought, he decided to include a few of them. He realized that his journey wasn't

KHALIL'S CLAY CREATIONS

just about successes; it was about embracing every part of the process, even the pieces that didn't feel perfect. They were part of his story, too.

Once he had selected the pieces, he began to think about how to arrange them. He wanted each piece to flow into the next, creating a story that viewers could follow as they moved through his display. He decided to arrange them in the order that he had created them, starting with his earliest works and moving toward his most recent pieces. This way, visitors could see his growth, his exploration of new techniques, and his journey toward finding his own voice in art.

As he set up the arrangement, he was struck by the visual story that emerged. His first pieces, with their traditional shapes and careful patterns, contrasted with the bold, abstract forms he had created later. It was like looking at a timeline of his experiences, his struggles, and his triumphs. Each piece held a memory, a lesson learned, and Khalil felt a surge of pride as he saw his journey come to life in front of him.

Mr. Simmons visited Khalil's space as he worked, nodding thoughtfully as he looked over the arrangement. "You've come a long way, Khalil," he said with a warm smile. "Your work has a voice now, a presence that's uniquely yours. I can see your journey, your growth, in every piece."

Khalil felt his heart swell with gratitude. He had always looked up to Mr. Simmons, and hearing those words meant the world to him. Mr. Simmons had guided him, encouraged him to push his boundaries, and now, standing here with his work on display, Khalil felt like he was honoring his teacher's belief in him.

Over the next few days, Khalil spent hours refining the details of his display, adjusting each piece, making sure everything was just right. He added small handwritten cards next to each piece, describing the inspiration behind it and the lessons he had learned. He wanted viewers to understand the story behind each work, to feel connected to his journey.

One evening, as he was working late at the studio, Aminah and Musa stopped by to check on his progress. They admired his display, nodding approvingly as they looked over his pieces.

"This is amazing, Khalil," Aminah said, her eyes bright with excitement. "I can see everything you've been through in each piece. It's like you're telling a story without words."

Musa added, "Yeah, your work really stands out. It's not just pottery—it's a reflection of who you are. You should be proud."

Khalil smiled, feeling a warmth spread through him. His friends had been by his side throughout this journey, sharing their own growth and learning experiences. He felt grateful for their support, for the inspiration they had given him, and he knew that this art show wasn't just his achievement—it was something they had all contributed to, a celebration of their shared journey.

In the final days leading up to the show, Khalil focused on preparing himself mentally and emotionally. He knew that displaying his work for others to see was a vulnerable experience, and he felt a mixture of excitement and anxiety at the thought of people walking through his display, examining each piece, interpreting his journey. He wondered what they would see, what they would feel. Would they understand the emotions, the memories, the experiences woven into each piece?

Khalil's grandmother visited him at the studio one day, her face filled with pride as she looked over his display. She examined each piece, taking her time, running her fingers along the textures and shapes, her eyes shining with admiration.

"This is beautiful, Khalil," she said softly, her voice filled with warmth. "Each piece tells a story, a part of your journey. I can see how much love and thought you put into every one."

Khalil felt his eyes sting with tears. His grandmother had been his greatest supporter, the one who had first encouraged him to find his own path in art. He hugged her tightly, feeling a deep gratitude for her wisdom, her guidance, and her belief in him.

Finally, the day of the art show arrived. Khalil woke up early, feeling a mixture of excitement and nervousness as he prepared himself for the big day. He dressed carefully, wanting to look his best, and headed to the studio, where his classmates were already busy with their own displays. The studio was transformed, filled with colors, shapes, and textures that reflected each artist's unique journey.

As the doors opened, a steady stream of visitors began to enter the space, wandering through the displays, admiring the variety of styles and forms. Khalil stood near his display, watching as people examined his work, reading the cards he had written, tracing the journey he had taken as an artist.

He watched as a young girl paused in front of his "perfectly imperfect" cup, her fingers lightly touching the small crack that ran along its side. Her mother read the card aloud, explaining how the piece symbolized the beauty of imperfection, of embracing flaws as part of the story. Khalil felt a surge of pride, knowing that his message was reaching others, that people were connecting with his work in a personal way.

Throughout the day, Khalil received feedback from visitors who were touched by his work, each person offering a new perspective, a unique interpretation of his pieces. Some people saw strength and resilience in his textured bowls, others felt a sense of peace in his abstract forms. Khalil was amazed at how each viewer brought their own experiences, their own emotions, to his work, creating a dialogue that went beyond words.

As the day went on, Khalil's friends and family stopped by to congratulate him, offering hugs and words of encouragement. His parents beamed with pride, his father's arm around his mother's shoulders as they admired his display. His friends were equally supportive, sharing their own reflections on his work, their appreciation for the journey they had witnessed alongside him.

Chapter 14: Reflecting on Success and Learning from Feedback

After the art show, Khalil felt a mixture of pride and relief. The event had been everything he'd hoped for and more—filled with people who genuinely connected with his work, family and friends who had shared in his success, and strangers who had found meaning in his pieces. For the first time, he felt like he could call himself an artist. But with the thrill of the show behind him, Khalil also found himself in a new phase: reflection. He knew he had grown through this experience, but he wondered what the next step would be, how he could build on everything he had learned and shared.

Over the next few days, Khalil visited the studio to take down his display. He worked carefully, almost reverently, as he packed each piece, remembering the emotions and memories attached to them. The art show had taught him so much about himself and his creative process, but he was also curious to know what others had thought about his work. As he packed, he thought back to the feedback he had received, recalling both the compliments and the observations people had shared. Some had admired the texture of his nature-inspired bowls; others had been moved by the abstract pieces that represented freedom and movement.

One comment in particular had stayed with him. A visitor had mentioned how his abstract wave reminded her of a journey, of riding through life's ups and downs. Khalil hadn't thought of it that way before, but he was fascinated by the idea. It made him realize that every viewer brought their own experiences and emotions to his work, seeing things that even he hadn't intended. It was as if each piece contained infinite interpretations, reflecting a part of both the creator and the viewer.

The feedback he received from Mr. Simmons was equally valuable. His teacher had taken time after the show to go through Khalil's pieces with him, sharing insights and observations that Khalil knew would stay with him for years to come. Mr. Simmons praised his courage for experimenting with different styles and techniques, for embracing his imperfections, and for pushing the boundaries of his own comfort zone. But he also encouraged Khalil to go further, to continue growing, and to remember that art was an endless journey of exploration.

One suggestion Mr. Simmons made stood out in Khalil's mind: he encouraged him to try working on larger pieces, to experiment with scale. Khalil's pottery so far had been relatively small, intimate pieces that people could hold and feel in their hands. But Mr. Simmons thought he might find new inspiration and challenges by creating larger works, pieces that would invite viewers to step back and experience them from a distance. The idea excited Khalil, though it also made him nervous. Larger pieces required different techniques, more clay, and, most of all, patience. It would be a new kind of challenge, one that he wasn't sure he was ready for, but one that he felt compelled to try.

With the encouragement of his friends, family, and Mr. Simmons, Khalil began planning his next steps. He decided to focus on the feedback he had received, to treat it as a guide that would help him move forward. He was particularly interested in exploring the theme of journeys, inspired by the visitor's comment on his wave piece. It struck him that his journey as an artist was still unfolding, that each piece was a step along the way, and he wanted his next creations to reflect that sense of growth and discovery.

Khalil began sketching ideas for larger pieces, drawing inspiration from the elements he had found most meaningful: nature, abstraction, and storytelling. He thought about the powerful sense of movement he had felt in his wave piece, the organic textures he had created to resemble rocks and trees, and the abstract forms that had allowed him to express emotions without words. His sketchbook filled with

KHALIL'S CLAY CREATIONS

ideas—large, sweeping forms that resembled waves, towering structures that felt like mountains, and spiraling shapes that seemed to flow and twist like rivers. He imagined how each piece might capture a different aspect of his journey, how they would invite viewers to see a part of themselves in the work.

His first attempt at a large piece was ambitious: a tall, twisting form that he imagined as a representation of resilience and strength. The shape was inspired by the old, gnarled trees he had seen in the forest, trees that had stood for centuries, weathering storms and seasons with quiet endurance. Khalil wanted the piece to capture that sense of endurance, to stand tall and proud, rooted in the earth yet reaching upward. As he worked, he realized that creating a large piece required a new kind of focus and patience. The clay was heavier, harder to shape, and every movement felt amplified.

He spent hours each day working on the piece, adjusting the curves, reinforcing the base, and smoothing out the surface. There were moments of frustration when the clay wouldn't cooperate or when a section collapsed under its own weight, but each setback became a lesson in resilience. He found himself thinking of the tree he was trying to capture, the way it had grown and thrived despite challenges. The piece slowly took shape, its form curving upward in a graceful twist that seemed to defy gravity. It felt like a testament to growth, to the strength it took to stand tall in the face of obstacles.

Once the piece was complete, Khalil felt a deep sense of accomplishment. He stepped back to admire it, seeing in it not just a tree, but a part of himself—his determination, his desire to grow, his resilience. He realized that the process of creating this piece had taught him as much as the finished work itself. The challenges, the setbacks, the small victories—they were all part of the journey, part of what made the piece meaningful.

Encouraged by the success of his first large piece, Khalil continued exploring the theme of journeys in his work. His next piece was inspired by rivers, by the way water flowed and adapted, carving its path through rock and earth. He imagined a piece that captured the sense of movement and change, a form that twisted and turned like a river winding through the landscape. As he worked, he thought about how each turn in the river represented a choice, a moment of decision. The piece became a reflection of his own journey, of the choices he had made as an artist, the paths he had taken and the ones he had left behind.

The river piece was more fluid and dynamic than the tree, its lines curving and intertwining in a way that invited viewers to follow its path. Khalil used a combination of textures to give the piece a sense of depth and movement, adding smooth areas to represent calm waters and rough sections to reflect the rapids and obstacles that rivers encounter. When he finished, he felt a sense of wonder at how the piece seemed to flow, how it captured the unpredictability of life, the way each choice shaped the path forward.

Chapter 15: Khalil's Experiment with Mixed Media

With each passing day, Khalil felt his confidence as an artist growing. He had ventured through the realms of shape, color, texture, and abstract expression, and he had even experimented with larger pieces that challenged his patience and skill. But now, a new idea was taking root in his mind—one that felt both thrilling and daunting. Khalil had always worked exclusively with clay, letting its natural, earthy qualities shape his creations. However, after hearing from his teacher, Mr. Simmons, about the power of mixed media, he found himself intrigued by the possibilities of combining clay with other materials. He imagined what his pottery might look like if it were woven together with wood, metal, or even glass. The thought opened up a new world of ideas, one he was eager to explore.

Mr. Simmons encouraged Khalil's curiosity and helped him get started by showing him some examples of mixed-media artwork, pieces that blended ceramics with elements like wood and metal. Khalil was particularly captivated by a sculpture that featured ceramic pieces interwoven with strands of copper wire, creating a striking contrast between the cool, polished metal and the warm, organic clay. The two materials, though vastly different, seemed to complement each other, each enhancing the other's qualities. Khalil felt inspired by the idea of using contrasting materials to create a sense of harmony, and he began to envision ways to incorporate mixed media into his own work.

His first experiment was a simple one. He decided to create a clay bowl and embed small pieces of glass into the surface, using broken bits of green and blue glass he had collected over time. He began by shaping the bowl, letting it take on a rounded form with gently sloping sides. Once he was satisfied with the shape, he carefully pressed the glass pieces into the clay, arranging them in a loose pattern around the rim.

The glass sparkled under the studio lights, creating a beautiful contrast against the rough, matte surface of the clay.

As he worked, Khalil realized that combining materials required a new level of precision. He had to be careful not to press the glass too deeply, as it could crack the clay or shift during firing. He also had to think about how the different materials would respond to heat. Glass and clay expanded at different rates, and he knew that if he wasn't careful, the glass might crack during firing. The process felt delicate and experimental, and Khalil enjoyed the challenge of balancing these new factors.

When the bowl was finally fired, Khalil was amazed at the result. The glass had melted slightly, bonding to the clay and creating a smooth, glossy surface that caught the light beautifully. The pieces of glass looked like tiny fragments of water, frozen in time against the earthy backdrop of the clay. Khalil felt a surge of excitement—he had successfully combined two materials in a way that felt natural, harmonious. The bowl felt alive, as if it held a piece of the earth and the sky within it.

Encouraged by his success, Khalil decided to push further. He began experimenting with wood, incorporating small wooden accents into his clay pieces. For his next project, he created a small, abstract sculpture with a wavy, flowing shape, inspired by the branches of trees and the gentle curves of riverbeds. Once the clay was fired and glazed, he attached thin wooden branches along the sides, using them to enhance the sense of movement in the piece. The wood brought a warmth and texture that complemented the smoothness of the clay, creating a sense of unity between the two materials.

As Khalil explored the possibilities of mixed media, he found himself learning new techniques and developing a deeper understanding of each material. Wood had its own natural textures and patterns, each piece unique in its grain and color. Metal, on the other hand, brought strength and resilience, but it required precision and care. Khalil started to see each material as a collaborator, each one adding its own voice, its own character, to the finished piece.

One of his favorite creations was a wall sculpture that combined clay, wood, and metal. He had crafted the clay into a series of organic, flowing shapes that resembled leaves or petals. Around these, he arranged small pieces of wood, their natural lines and textures creating a sense of movement. To add contrast, he used thin copper wires to connect the pieces, weaving the metal through the wood and clay in a delicate, intricate pattern. The copper gleamed against the muted tones of the clay and wood, adding a sense of energy and vitality to the piece.

The finished sculpture felt like a celebration of nature, a tribute to the different elements that made up the world around him. Each material brought its own qualities, yet together they created a sense of harmony, a balance that felt both natural and intentional. Khalil felt a deep sense of satisfaction, knowing that he had created something unique, something that reflected his journey as an artist and his desire to push boundaries.

But working with mixed media wasn't always easy. There were times when the materials didn't cooperate, when the clay wouldn't bond with the wood or the metal wouldn't bend the way he wanted. He faced moments of frustration, especially when pieces broke or cracked during the firing process. But each challenge taught him something new, forcing him to adapt, to find creative solutions, to work with the materials rather than against them.

One day, while experimenting with a new piece that combined clay and metal, Khalil faced a setback. He had designed a small sculpture with metal rods embedded into the clay, each rod curving upward like a tree branch. But during firing, the rods expanded, causing cracks to form in the clay. Khalil felt disappointed, seeing his vision crumble in front of him. But Mr. Simmons reminded him that setbacks were part of the creative process, that each failure was an opportunity to learn and grow. Taking his teacher's advice to heart, Khalil reworked the piece, adjusting the placement of the rods and reinforcing the clay to better handle the pressure. The finished sculpture wasn't exactly as he had envisioned, but it held a strength and resilience that came from overcoming the challenges he had faced.

As Khalil continued to explore mixed media, he found that each material had its own voice, its own personality. Clay was earthy and grounding, full of potential for texture and form. Wood was warm and organic, its natural patterns telling a story of growth and time. Metal was strong yet pliable, adding structure and contrast. And glass was delicate and fragile, bringing light and color. Each material felt like a character in his work, each one bringing its own qualities to the story he was trying to tell.

Through these experiments, Khalil learned the importance of balance, of knowing when to let each material take the lead and when to step back. He began to see his role as a guide, helping the materials find their place, their harmony within the piece. The process required patience, intuition, and a willingness to listen to what each material needed, to allow the piece to unfold naturally.

One of his most ambitious projects was a large mixed-media sculpture inspired by the elements of earth, air, fire, and water. Khalil wanted each element to be represented by a different material: clay for earth, metal for fire, wood for air, and glass for water. He envisioned a piece that would capture the energy and balance of these elements, a piece that would feel alive, dynamic, filled with movement.

He began by shaping the clay into a sturdy base, its texture rough and earthy, like stone. From there, he added metal rods that twisted upward, representing fire with their strength and intensity. Thin branches of wood extended from the top, creating a sense of lightness, of air. Finally, he incorporated pieces of blue and green glass, arranging them along the surface like droplets of water.

The finished piece was unlike anything he had ever created. It felt both powerful and delicate, grounded yet reaching upward, a reflection of the natural world and the balance within it. Khalil felt a deep sense of accomplishment as he looked at the sculpture, knowing that he had created something that celebrated the harmony of different elements, different materials. He had woven together clay, metal, wood, and glass, each one contributing its own qualities, its own beauty.

Through his exploration of mixed media, Khalil had discovered a new way of seeing his art, a new way of expressing his vision. He realized that art didn't have to be confined to one material, one form. It could be a collaboration, a dialogue between different elements, each one adding depth and complexity to the final piece. He felt a sense of freedom, a belief that he could continue to grow, to push the boundaries of his creativity.

Chapter 16: Teaching Others

As Khalil's journey with pottery continued, he found himself drawn to a new idea that he hadn't considered before: sharing what he had learned with others. Up until now, he had been the student, learning from Mr. Simmons, from his friends, and from his own experiences. But recently, he had started to think about how much he had grown, how much he had discovered, and the idea of helping others start their own journeys felt meaningful and exciting. He wanted to pass along the passion and knowledge that had transformed his life, to see how he might inspire others to discover the beauty of art and creativity.

One afternoon, Khalil brought up the idea with Mr. Simmons, wondering if he might be ready to take on such a role. He explained that he wanted to help newcomers find their own voices, just as he had found his. Mr. Simmons listened thoughtfully, a warm smile on his face, and he nodded in agreement. He mentioned that a group of younger students had recently expressed interest in learning pottery, and he suggested that Khalil could lead a workshop for them.

Khalil felt both thrilled and nervous at the thought. He had never taught anyone before, and he wasn't sure if he could convey what he had learned in a way that would be helpful. But the more he thought about it, the more excited he became. He knew what it felt like to be a beginner, to feel uncertain and curious, and he wanted to help guide these students in a way that felt supportive and encouraging. He spent the next few days preparing for the workshop, planning activities that would introduce the students to the basics of pottery and give them a taste of the creativity it offered.

When the day of the workshop arrived, Khalil welcomed a small group of eager students into the studio. They ranged in age from ten to fourteen, and each one seemed to be filled with a mixture of excitement and curiosity. Some of them looked around the studio wide-eyed, marveling at the tools, the wheels, and the shelves lined with finished pieces. Khalil felt a surge of pride as he watched them; he remembered his own first day in the studio, the sense of wonder and possibility that had filled him, and he wanted these students to feel the same excitement.

He began by introducing himself, sharing a little about his journey with pottery, the challenges he had faced, and the joy he had found in creating. He could see their faces light up as he talked, their curiosity piqued by the idea that they, too, could create something meaningful. He then explained the basics, showing them how to prepare the clay, how to form it into a simple shape, and how to use the pottery wheel.

As he demonstrated each step, he encouraged them to ask questions, to experiment, and not to worry about making mistakes. He wanted them to feel free to explore, to play with the clay, and to trust their instincts. Some of the students were hesitant at first, nervous about the unfamiliar tools and materials. But Khalil took the time to guide each one individually, showing them how to shape the clay, how to feel its texture, and how to let their hands move naturally.

One of the students, a young girl named Sara, struggled with the wheel, her hands trembling as she tried to center the clay. Khalil knelt beside her, patiently explaining how to keep her hands steady, how to find the right balance of pressure. He could see her frustration melting into concentration as she followed his guidance, her hands finally finding a rhythm on the wheel. The clay began to take shape under her fingers, transforming into a small, simple bowl. When she looked up, her face was filled with pride, a beaming smile that reminded Khalil of his own early triumphs. He felt a deep sense of fulfillment, knowing he had helped her experience that moment of discovery.

As the class continued, Khalil introduced the students to some of the techniques he had learned over the years, from adding texture to experimenting with different shapes. He shared stories about his own creations, about the times he had struggled with a piece or found inspiration in unexpected places. He wanted them to see that art wasn't just about creating something beautiful; it was about expressing themselves, capturing moments and emotions in a way that was unique to each person.

The students responded with enthusiasm, their imaginations sparked by his stories and examples. One boy, named Alex, became fascinated by the idea of abstract shapes and decided to create a piece that didn't follow any traditional form. He shaped his clay into a twisting, flowing design, experimenting with lines and angles. Khalil encouraged him to keep going, to let his creativity guide him. When Alex finished, his piece looked like a small wave, full of movement and energy. Khalil admired the courage it took to step outside the familiar, and he praised Alex for embracing his own vision.

Another student, Maya, was drawn to texture, inspired by Khalil's stories of using natural materials to add depth to his work. She carefully pressed leaves into her clay, creating delicate imprints that gave her piece a sense of nature and growth. Khalil was impressed by her attention to detail, by the way she had embraced the idea of using texture to tell a story. He praised her work, encouraging her to keep experimenting, to keep exploring the possibilities that clay offered.

As the workshop continued, Khalil found himself fully immersed in the joy of teaching. He loved seeing the students discover their own styles, their own voices. Each one approached the clay differently, bringing their personalities and perspectives into their work. He realized that teaching was more than just sharing techniques; it was about nurturing their confidence, helping them find a path that felt true to them.

By the end of the day, the students had created a collection of pieces that reflected their individual styles, their unique voices. Some had crafted simple, delicate bowls, others had made abstract shapes, and a few had added textures and patterns that captured moments of inspiration. Khalil was moved by the diversity of their work, by the way each piece told a different story. He knew that these students had just taken their first steps on a journey that could last a lifetime, a journey filled with discovery, growth, and self-expression.

As the students packed up their pieces and prepared to leave, Khalil gathered them together for a final reflection. He thanked them for their enthusiasm, for their willingness to try something new, and he encouraged them to keep creating, to keep exploring their creativity. He reminded them that art wasn't about perfection; it was about expressing themselves, about finding joy in the process. He could see the excitement in their eyes, the spark of inspiration that he knew would stay with them long after the workshop ended.

In the days that followed, Khalil found himself reflecting on the experience, on how much he had enjoyed teaching, on how fulfilling it had been to share his passion with others. He felt a deep sense of gratitude for the journey that had brought him here, for the people who had guided him, for the lessons he had learned. Teaching had given him a new perspective, a reminder of the joy and wonder that came with being a beginner, of the courage it took to try something new.

He realized that teaching was its own form of art, one that required patience, empathy, and an open heart. He had to listen, to understand each student's needs and goals, to guide them without imposing his own vision. He found joy in watching them discover their own paths, in seeing their confidence grow, in knowing that he had been a small part of their journey.

Through teaching, Khalil gained a deeper understanding of his own work, of the lessons he had learned along the way. He realized that each piece he had created, each challenge he had faced, each breakthrough he had experienced, had prepared him for this moment. Teaching had become a new chapter in his journey, a way of giving back, of honoring the teachers and mentors who had inspired him.

Chapter 17: Khalil's Artistic Identity

As Khalil's journey continued, he felt himself reaching a turning point. Teaching others had opened his eyes to a deeper understanding of his craft, and each day he grew more aware of the evolution of his own artistic identity. But as rewarding as his experiences had been, Khalil was starting to feel a pull toward something more, a desire to solidify his unique style, to fully embrace the artist he was becoming. He wanted to create work that was unmistakably his, pieces that would reflect his journey, his experiences, and his unique perspective. He realized that he wanted people to see a piece of pottery and know that it was a "Khalil," not just by sight but by the feeling it evoked.

To begin this search for identity, Khalil knew he had to spend time alone with his thoughts and his art. While he loved teaching and sharing the studio with others, he needed space to reflect, to dig deep into what art truly meant to him. So, he decided to take a few weeks to work on his own, spending time in quiet introspection, thinking about what made his work unique. He remembered how his grandmother had encouraged him to embrace his own voice, to create art that reflected his personality, his beliefs, and his journey. This advice had been a guiding light for him, but now he wanted to understand it on a deeper level.

Khalil began by looking back at his previous work, reviewing each piece, each style he had explored. He saw the early pieces where he had focused on traditional forms, bowls and vases with smooth surfaces and simple glazes. He admired their simplicity but realized that they lacked the sense of expression that he now sought. Moving forward, he could see how his experimentation with color, texture, and abstract forms had brought new life into his work, how each phase of his journey had added a layer to his understanding of art. He saw the evolution from careful, predictable shapes to bold, organic forms, from neat patterns to wild, flowing lines. Each piece was a stepping stone, a part of the larger picture of who he was as an artist.

One day, as he sat in his small studio, he allowed himself to imagine what he wanted his art to say. He thought about the themes that resonated with him: nature, resilience, growth, and the beauty of imperfection. He realized that his journey with pottery had been a journey of self-discovery, and he wanted his art to reflect that. He wanted his pieces to feel alive, to capture moments of change and growth, to embody the raw beauty of nature and life's unexpected paths. He wanted his pottery to tell a story, to invite viewers to see something of themselves in each piece.

With these ideas in mind, Khalil began experimenting with a new series of works that would serve as a personal reflection, a collection that represented the core of his artistic identity. His first piece was inspired by the concept of resilience, a theme that had always been close to his heart. He envisioned a sculpture that captured the strength and endurance he saw in nature, in the way trees grew around obstacles, in the way rivers carved their paths through stone. The piece would be a testament to the power of resilience, to the idea that growth could come from struggle.

He began by shaping a tall, twisting form with rough, jagged edges. The clay was thick and heavy, giving the piece a sense of strength, of being rooted in the earth. He added texture to the surface, pressing in lines and ridges that mimicked the bark of an ancient tree. As he worked, he found himself pouring his own experiences into the clay—the times he had struggled, the challenges he had faced and overcome. The finished piece stood tall and proud, its surface scarred yet beautiful, a symbol of resilience and strength.

Looking at the sculpture, Khalil felt a deep sense of connection to it. He realized that he had created something that reflected his journey, a piece that held a part of his story. It was a representation of his growth, his determination, and his belief in the beauty of imperfection.

This piece, he felt, was a part of his identity, a piece that spoke of who he was as an artist and as a person.

Encouraged by this discovery, Khalil continued creating pieces that reflected his personal themes. His next piece was inspired by the idea of interconnectedness, by the belief that all life was connected, that we were all part of a larger whole. He thought about the relationships he had formed with his friends, his family, his teacher, and even the students he had taught. Each connection had shaped him, had helped him grow, and he wanted to capture that sense of unity, of belonging, in his work.

He began by crafting a series of small, circular shapes that he connected to form a larger whole. Each circle was unique, with its own texture, its own color, but together they formed a cohesive piece. Khalil chose earthy tones, greens and browns and blues, colors that reminded him of nature, of the land, the sky, the sea. The finished piece looked like a mosaic, each small shape representing a connection, a part of the larger picture. He felt a sense of peace as he looked at it, a reminder that he was never alone on his journey, that each person who had touched his life was a part of his story.

As he continued working on this series, Khalil found himself growing more confident in his artistic voice. Each piece felt like a revelation, a step closer to understanding who he was as an artist. He experimented with different forms and materials, incorporating elements from his past work—textures inspired by nature, abstract shapes, bold colors. He allowed himself to be guided by his instincts, to create pieces that felt true to him, pieces that carried a part of his heart.

One of his favorite pieces from this series was a bowl with a cracked surface, inspired by the concept of vulnerability. Khalil wanted to capture the beauty of imperfection, to show that flaws could be a source of strength, that brokenness didn't diminish beauty but added to it. He shaped the bowl with care, creating a smooth, delicate surface, then intentionally added small cracks and imperfections. He filled each

KHALIL'S CLAY CREATIONS

crack with a gold glaze, creating a contrast that highlighted the flaws rather than hiding them. The finished piece was both fragile and beautiful, a reminder that vulnerability was a part of life, that strength could be found in embracing one's imperfections.

Khalil's studio became a space of discovery and expression, a place where he could explore the depths of his identity, where he could create work that reflected his heart. Each piece became a part of his journey, a marker of his growth, a testament to his belief in the power of art. He found joy in the process, a sense of fulfillment that came from creating work that felt true, work that was a part of him.

As his series grew, Khalil began to feel a sense of completion, a belief that he had found something meaningful, something that captured the essence of who he was. He knew that his artistic identity would continue to evolve, that he would keep growing, keep learning. But for now, he felt at peace, knowing that he had created work that spoke of his journey, that held a piece of his soul.

One day, Mr. Simmons visited Khalil's studio, admiring the new pieces he had created. He looked over each one carefully, nodding with approval, his eyes filled with pride. "Khalil, you've found your voice," he said softly, placing a hand on Khalil's shoulder. "These pieces… they're you. They reflect your journey, your heart. You've created something truly beautiful."

With his series complete, Khalil decided to hold a small exhibition, inviting his friends, family, and community to see the work he had created. The pieces were arranged in a way that told his story, each one representing a part of his journey, a reflection of his growth. As people moved through the exhibition, Khalil watched their reactions, their smiles, their thoughtful expressions. He felt a sense of pride, a belief that he had created something meaningful, something that connected with others.

At the end of the evening, Khalil's grandmother hugged him tightly, her eyes filled with pride. "You've become an artist, Khalil," she whispered. "You've found your voice. And it's beautiful."

Khalil smiled, feeling a deep sense of peace, a belief that he had found something true. He knew that his journey would continue, that he would keep growing, keep exploring, keep creating. But for now, he felt complete, knowing that he had found his place, that he had created art that was a reflection of his heart, his soul, his journey.

Chapter 18: A Collaborative Project with the Community

With a renewed sense of purpose in his art and a deeper understanding of his identity, Khalil felt fulfilled but also ready for his next challenge. He had grown as an individual artist, developing his voice, creating work that resonated with his journey, and even teaching others. But he felt a growing urge to step outside of himself, to create something that wasn't just a personal reflection but also a collaboration, a piece that represented his entire community. Inspired by the support his friends and family had shown him, Khalil wanted to create something that could bring everyone together, a project that would capture the essence of his neighborhood and the people who had shaped his life.

One morning, as he walked through the neighborhood, Khalil noticed how each shop, each park, each home carried its own character and history. He thought about the people he saw every day—the neighbors, the shopkeepers, the families who gathered in the park—and realized that each person held a story. He envisioned a project that would celebrate these stories, a piece of art that would embody the diversity, resilience, and unity of his community. After spending hours brainstorming, he decided he wanted to create a large mural using ceramic tiles. Each tile would represent a part of his neighborhood, and he hoped to invite community members to contribute their own designs to make it a true collaborative work.

Khalil eagerly approached Mr. Simmons with his idea, seeking guidance on how to bring it to life. Mr. Simmons was thrilled, seeing in Khalil's plan a beautiful opportunity for both community-building and artistic expression. They discussed logistics, considering the space needed, the time it would take, and the resources required. Khalil wanted the mural to be displayed in a public area, somewhere people could see it every day. With Mr. Simmons's encouragement, Khalil decided to reach out to the local community center to propose his idea.

After a few phone calls and meetings, Khalil presented his vision to the community center's directors. He explained how each tile would represent a part of the neighborhood, that he wanted to invite people of all ages and backgrounds to contribute to the design. The directors were excited by the idea, appreciating the opportunity to bring people together through art. They offered him a large wall in the center's entrance, a place where everyone who visited could see the mural and feel a part of it.

With a location secured, Khalil set to work organizing the project. He decided to divide the mural into sections, with each section representing a different aspect of the community: family, nature, local businesses, and cultural diversity. He hoped that these themes would resonate with everyone, that each person who participated would find a way to express their own connection to the neighborhood. He created a sign-up sheet at the community center and put up posters around the neighborhood, inviting people to join the project and share their stories through art.

In the weeks that followed, people from all walks of life signed up to participate. Khalil was amazed by the diversity of those who came forward: children, parents, elderly residents, business owners, and even people from the local park who had heard about the project. Each person brought their own perspective, their own story, and Khalil felt a deep sense of gratitude as he welcomed them into the studio.

He organized the participants into small groups, giving each group a section of the mural to work on. Some groups focused on family, creating tiles that depicted scenes of gatherings, meals, and celebrations. Others focused on nature, crafting tiles with trees, flowers, and animals. Khalil encouraged each person to bring their own ideas, to feel free to express themselves through color, shape, and texture. The studio was filled with energy and excitement as people sketched designs, shaped clay, and added glazes. Khalil moved between the groups, offering guidance, sharing techniques, and encouraging each person to explore their creativity.

One of the most touching moments came when an elderly woman named Laila joined the project. She had lived in the neighborhood for over fifty years and had seen it change and grow over the decades. She wanted to create a tile that represented her memories of the neighborhood, the people she had known, the places that had disappeared over time. She sketched a small park that used to be the heart of the community, a place where children had played and families had gathered. Her tile was simple, yet filled with warmth and nostalgia, a reminder of the neighborhood's history and the people who had been part of it.

Khalil was moved by Laila's tile, by the sense of history it captured, and he encouraged her to share her memories with the younger participants. She spent time with the children, telling them stories about the neighborhood's past, about the people and places that had shaped it. The children listened with wide eyes, fascinated by the history of their home, by the stories that had been passed down through generations. Khalil realized that this project was doing more than just creating art; it was building connections, bridging generations, and bringing people together in a way he hadn't expected.

Another group of participants consisted of local business owners who wanted to celebrate the spirit of entrepreneurship that had shaped the neighborhood. They created tiles that represented their businesses—a small bakery, a family-owned bookstore, a barber shop that had been in the community for decades. Each tile captured the unique character of the business, from the warm glow of the bakery's ovens to the cozy shelves of the bookstore. Khalil was inspired by their pride, by the sense of dedication and love they felt for their work. He realized that the neighborhood was not just a place; it was a community built on the hard work and dreams of the people who lived there.

As the mural began to take shape, Khalil could see the diversity and richness of the community coming to life. Each tile told a story, each section represented a piece of the neighborhood's identity. The tiles were filled with vibrant colors, textures, and patterns, a patchwork of experiences and memories that reflected the spirit of the community. Khalil felt a deep sense of pride as he watched people working together, sharing their stories, laughing, and connecting. The mural was becoming a symbol of unity, a celebration of the people who made the neighborhood what it was.

The project continued over several weeks, with new participants joining each day. Khalil noticed how the mural brought people together, how strangers became friends, how people from different backgrounds found common ground in their love for their home. He felt a deep sense of fulfillment, knowing that he had helped create something meaningful, something that would bring people together long after the mural was finished.

Chapter 19: Exploring Cultural Symbolism in Art

After completing the community mural, Khalil found himself reflecting on the many influences that had shaped his journey as an artist. He thought about the stories he had heard, the people he had met, and the rich history woven into the fabric of his neighborhood. The mural had opened his eyes to the diversity and beauty of the cultures around him, and he realized that his next chapter might involve exploring these cultural elements more deeply. Khalil wanted to create art that celebrated cultural symbols, that told stories from across the world, that honored the customs, beliefs, and shared human experiences that had stood the test of time. This idea felt daunting yet exhilarating, and he knew it would require him to approach his art with sensitivity, respect, and openness.

Khalil began by doing research, immersing himself in the stories and symbols of different cultures. He visited the library, borrowed books on art history and cultural symbols, and read about the ancient meanings behind various forms, colors, and patterns. The journey was eye-opening; he discovered how certain shapes carried spiritual meanings, how colors symbolized emotions or elements, and how simple lines or designs could tell complex stories. He learned that some symbols represented universal ideas—love, resilience, growth—while others reflected the unique beliefs and values of specific communities.

One symbol that captured Khalil's attention was the circle, which he discovered was a powerful symbol across many cultures. In some traditions, the circle represented unity, the cycle of life, and eternity. Khalil thought about how the circle also related to his own journey, the idea that life was a series of interconnected moments, each one leading to the next. Inspired, he decided to create a piece that would celebrate this universal symbol, capturing its essence in a way that reflected both its cultural significance and his personal journey.

He began by shaping a large, circular platter, allowing the clay to take on a smooth, balanced form. Once he was satisfied with the shape, he carefully etched patterns around the edge of the circle, drawing inspiration from traditional designs he had seen in his research. He added small details that reflected the interconnectedness of life—spirals, waves, and dots, each element flowing into the next. The piece felt timeless, as if it were part of a larger story, a tribute to the shared human experience that the circle represented.

As he worked, Khalil felt a sense of reverence for the stories behind the symbols he was using. He wanted to ensure that he was honoring their origins, that he was creating something that celebrated rather than appropriated. He reached out to friends, asking for their perspectives, seeking to understand how different cultures viewed these symbols. The conversations were enlightening; each friend shared their own understanding, their own connection to the symbols, adding depth and meaning to Khalil's work.

One day, while discussing cultural symbols with his grandmother, she shared with him the meaning of the moon in their family's tradition. She explained that in her culture, the moon represented change, intuition, and the passing of time. The moon was seen as a guiding light, a reminder that life was always in motion, that each phase carried its own beauty and challenges. Khalil was captivated by the idea, and he decided to create a series of pieces inspired by the phases of the moon, capturing the sense of transformation and growth that his grandmother had described.

He began by crafting small bowls, each one representing a different phase of the moon—new, waxing, full, and waning. He used different glazes to capture the changing light of the moon, from soft silvers to deep, shadowy blues. Each bowl was unique, reflecting the subtle differences of each phase, yet together they formed a cohesive whole.

Khalil felt a sense of wonder as he completed the series, realizing that he had created something that honored his grandmother's teachings, that captured the beauty of change and the passage of time.

As he continued exploring cultural symbols, Khalil found himself drawn to symbols of strength and resilience, ideas that resonated deeply with his own journey. One symbol that stood out was the tree, a powerful representation of life, growth, and endurance in many cultures. He read about the symbolism of trees in ancient myths, learning how they were often seen as connections between heaven and earth, rooted in the ground yet reaching for the sky. Khalil felt a strong connection to this idea; it reminded him of his own journey, of his desire to grow, to reach beyond his comfort zone while staying grounded.

Inspired, Khalil decided to create a tree sculpture that would capture the strength and resilience of nature. He envisioned a piece with strong, twisting branches, a trunk that seemed to grow and change with each curve, roots that spread wide and deep. He wanted the sculpture to feel alive, to capture the sense of movement and growth he saw in the tree symbol. He spent hours working on the piece, shaping each branch, carving intricate details into the bark, adding texture and depth to the roots. The finished sculpture felt like a testament to resilience, a reminder of the strength that came from staying rooted while reaching upward.

The process of exploring cultural symbols became deeply meaningful for Khalil, a journey of understanding and respect. He realized that these symbols were more than just designs or shapes; they were carriers of stories, vessels of history, reminders of the beliefs and values that had shaped human life for centuries. He felt honored to incorporate them into his work, to create pieces that celebrated the diversity and unity of human experience.

As he shared his pieces with friends and family, Khalil was touched by their reactions. Each person seemed to connect with the symbols in their own way, finding personal meanings, memories, or reflections in the art. His grandmother was particularly moved by the moon series, seeing in it a tribute to her teachings, a continuation of the family's tradition. Khalil felt a deep sense of fulfillment, knowing that he had created something meaningful, something that connected his personal journey to the broader human experience.

One of Khalil's friends, a potter from another neighborhood, invited him to participate in a cultural art fair, where artists from different backgrounds would share work that celebrated their heritage and inspirations. Khalil eagerly accepted, seeing it as an opportunity to showcase his new series, to share the cultural symbols he had learned about and honored in his work. He carefully selected pieces from his collection, choosing those that best represented the themes of unity, resilience, and transformation.

At the fair, Khalil's display drew visitors from all walks of life, each person drawn to the symbols and stories embedded in his pottery. He watched as people admired the circle platter, the moon bowls, and the tree sculpture, their faces filled with curiosity and wonder. Some people recognized the symbols from their own cultures, while others asked questions, wanting to learn about the meanings behind each piece. Khalil was moved by the conversations, by the way people shared their own stories, their own connections to the symbols.

One elderly man approached Khalil's display, his eyes lighting up as he recognized the circle design. He explained that in his culture, the circle was a symbol of protection, a shape that represented the family, the community, the bonds that held people together. Khalil listened intently, grateful for the insight, feeling a sense of connection to the man's story. He realized that the symbols he had used were not just abstract ideas; they were living connections, reminders of the shared human experience.

Chapter 20: Experimenting with New Forms

With the art fair behind him and a fresh sense of purpose from his exploration of cultural symbolism, Khalil felt ready to embark on yet another new journey. This time, he wanted to experiment with the very forms and structures of his pottery. For so long, he had been working with bowls, vases, and sculptures, but he wondered what would happen if he broke away from tradition and created forms that defied conventional shapes. He wanted his pieces to feel as if they were alive, to challenge the viewer's perception, to show that pottery didn't have to be confined to expected forms but could reflect the fluid, unpredictable nature of life itself.

As he thought about the project, Khalil felt a mixture of excitement and uncertainty. He had been comfortable with certain shapes and forms, with pieces that were recognizable, functional, and beautiful. But the idea of creating something unexpected, something abstract and unfamiliar, sparked a thrill in him. He decided to let go of any expectations, to embrace the freedom of creation without limitations. His goal was to explore the idea of movement, to create pottery that captured motion, that felt as if it were flowing, twisting, or even suspended in time.

To start, Khalil spent hours sketching, allowing his mind to wander, letting the lines on the paper take on shapes he had never considered before. He drew spirals that twisted inwards, shapes that curved and looped, structures that seemed to grow in multiple directions at once. He filled pages with these sketches, each one more daring than the last. Some shapes looked like waves frozen mid-crest, others like tree branches reaching and curling, while others seemed to resemble forms he couldn't even name. These shapes were unlike anything he had created before, and as he looked over the sketches, he felt a renewed sense of possibility.

Khalil began with a shape that resembled a wave, a form that would flow upwards in a twisting spiral, each curve leading to the next. He started shaping the clay slowly, letting his hands follow the movement he envisioned. This piece was challenging from the very beginning; without the stability of a traditional shape, he had to carefully balance each curve, making sure the form didn't collapse under its own weight. He found himself constantly adjusting, tweaking the angles, adding support in places where the clay felt vulnerable. As he worked, he realized that creating movement in clay was not just about the shape itself, but also about understanding the balance and flow within the piece.

Once the wave was shaped, Khalil faced another challenge—glazing. He wanted the colors to add depth and emphasize the movement of the piece. He chose a gradient of blues and greens, layering them in a way that would mimic the colors of the ocean, darker at the base and gradually lightening as it spiraled upwards. He carefully applied each layer of glaze, blending the colors together to create a seamless flow. When the piece was finally fired, the colors had fused into a beautiful gradient, giving the wave a sense of fluidity and life. Khalil was thrilled with the result; he had captured a moment of motion, a piece that felt as if it were reaching upward, caught in a continuous spiral.

Encouraged by his success, Khalil decided to push even further. His next piece was inspired by the idea of roots growing and intertwining, a form that would feel grounded yet dynamic. He envisioned a structure that twisted and spread out, with tendrils of clay reaching in multiple directions. The piece would represent growth, resilience, and the interconnectedness of life, a reminder of the strength that came from being rooted.

Shaping this piece required patience and care. Each tendril had to be shaped individually, then attached to the main structure, creating a network of roots that felt organic and alive. The clay needed to be firm enough to hold its shape but malleable enough to blend seamlessly into the other tendrils. Khalil spent hours working on each section, adding texture to the surface to mimic the rough, uneven quality of real roots. He experimented with different glazes, choosing earthy tones that would enhance the natural feel of the piece. When the piece was fired, it looked like a living structure, a network of roots reaching out and intertwining. Khalil was amazed by the sense of movement he had captured, the way the piece seemed to grow and expand.

His exploration of new forms continued, each piece challenging him to think differently, to approach clay as a medium of motion rather than stillness. He began working on shapes that resembled spirals, loops, and twists, experimenting with different textures and colors to enhance the feeling of movement. One piece, inspired by the image of a leaf caught in a gust of wind, took on a delicate, flowing shape with thin, curling edges that seemed to ripple in the air. Khalil spent days refining the piece, making sure each curve and twist looked natural, that the clay felt as if it were caught in motion. The final piece was fragile yet dynamic, a reminder of the beauty in fleeting moments.

As he continued creating these new forms, Khalil realized that he was discovering something profound about his art. By breaking away from traditional shapes, he was challenging himself to see clay in a new light, to embrace its potential for expression and movement. He felt a sense of freedom in creating these pieces, a feeling of joy in exploring the unknown. Each piece became a journey, an opportunity to push the boundaries of what pottery could be.

One day, as Khalil worked on a particularly intricate piece inspired by the branches of a tree, he received a visit from Mr. Simmons, who had heard about his experiments with new forms. Mr. Simmons was fascinated by Khalil's work, admiring the sense of movement, the way each piece seemed to defy gravity, to flow and twist in unexpected ways. He praised Khalil for his courage, for his willingness to break free from convention, to explore the possibilities of clay as a medium of expression.

Khalil was grateful for his teacher's support, for the encouragement that had been a guiding light throughout his journey. He shared with Mr. Simmons the challenges he had faced in creating these pieces, the struggle to find balance, the difficulty of capturing motion in a medium that was traditionally still. Mr. Simmons listened with interest, offering insights and suggestions, reminding Khalil that art was as much about the process as the final product.

Inspired by his conversation with Mr. Simmons, Khalil decided to take his exploration even further. He began experimenting with mixed media, incorporating metal and glass into his forms to add depth and contrast. In one piece, he combined clay with thin, curved metal rods that extended from the structure, creating the illusion of movement beyond the clay itself. The metal added a sense of lightness, a contrast to the solidity of the clay, enhancing the feeling of motion. Khalil was thrilled with the result, feeling as if he had created something truly unique, a piece that blended strength with delicacy, stillness with movement.

Another piece featured glass elements embedded within the clay, small pieces that sparkled and reflected light, adding a sense of energy to the form. Khalil loved the way the glass captured the light, the way it interacted with the clay, creating a piece that felt alive. He realized that by combining materials, he could add new dimensions to his work, creating pieces that were not only visually striking but also deeply expressive.

As he continued to experiment, Khalil found himself drawn to the idea of transformation, of creating pieces that seemed to evolve, to change as they were viewed from different angles. He worked on a large, spiral structure that appeared differently from every side, each curve and twist revealing a new shape, a new perspective. The piece became a symbol of change, a reminder that life was always in motion, that each moment was a step in a continuous journey.

When he finally completed the series, Khalil felt a deep sense of accomplishment. Each piece represented a part of his journey, a reflection of his desire to push boundaries, to explore the unknown. He knew that these pieces were unlike anything he had created before, that they represented a new chapter in his artistic journey. He decided to display them in a local gallery, hoping to share his exploration of movement and transformation with others.

The gallery opening was a success, drawing people from all over the community who were fascinated by Khalil's work. Visitors moved through the display, admiring the pieces, discussing the sense of movement and change that each one evoked. Khalil watched as people reacted to the forms, each person bringing their own perspective, their own interpretation. Some saw waves, others saw trees or roots, while others found meanings that Khalil hadn't even considered.

Chapter 21: Khalil's Journey into Functional Art

With each exploration into new forms and styles, Khalil found himself circling back to a question that had been lingering in his mind: what role did functionality play in his art? So many of his recent works had been abstract, experimental, and expressive, yet the origins of pottery lay in functional pieces—objects that people could use in their everyday lives. Khalil began to wonder if he could create pieces that were both functional and meaningful, pieces that people could not only admire but also interact with daily. The idea of bringing art into people's lives in a tangible way felt both challenging and exciting, and Khalil knew he was ready to explore it.

The inspiration for his first project came from a family dinner. As Khalil set the table with his mother's traditional dishes, he thought about how certain objects held memories, how even a simple bowl or plate could carry a history of shared meals and moments. He wanted to create pieces that people could use every day, objects that would become part of their lives, part of their routines, and part of their own stories. This idea excited him, and he envisioned creating a collection of functional pottery that reflected the themes he held close to his heart: connection, unity, and celebration.

Khalil decided to start with a set of bowls, each one unique yet part of a larger collection. He wanted each bowl to feel like a small piece of art, something that people could admire as much as they could use. He thought about the forms he had explored in his previous work, the curves, textures, and colors, and wondered how he could bring those elements into functional pieces without compromising their usability. The challenge lay in finding the right balance, creating pieces that were both beautiful and practical.

He began by shaping the clay, experimenting with different forms until he found a shape that felt right. The bowls were slightly asymmetrical, with gentle curves that gave them a natural, organic feel. Khalil wanted them to look as if they had been shaped by nature, like stones polished by water over time. He added subtle textures to the surface, pressing in patterns inspired by leaves, waves, and tree bark, creating a tactile quality that invited people to touch and explore.

When it came to glazing, Khalil decided to use earthy colors, blending shades of green, brown, and blue to create a natural palette. He wanted the colors to feel soothing, to remind people of nature, of the earth. He spent hours experimenting with different techniques, layering glazes to achieve a depth and richness that would enhance the textures he had created. The result was a collection of bowls that felt both earthy and elegant, each one unique yet connected to the others in a cohesive design.

As he completed the bowls, Khalil felt a sense of accomplishment. He had created pieces that were not only beautiful but also functional, objects that people could hold, use, and appreciate. He imagined these bowls becoming part of someone's daily routine, used for morning cereal, evening soup, or a late-night snack. He imagined them holding memories, becoming part of someone's life in a way that his purely artistic pieces couldn't.

Encouraged by the success of the bowls, Khalil decided to expand his collection to include other functional pieces. He created a series of mugs, each one with a unique handle that fit comfortably in the hand, designed to invite people to hold them, to feel the warmth of a hot drink on a cold morning. He shaped the mugs with a slight curve, giving them a comfortable, balanced feel, and added textures that echoed the designs in his bowls. He chose colors that felt warm and inviting, a mix of deep reds, browns, and soft greens.

Each mug felt like a personal invitation, a piece that someone could connect with, that could become part of their daily ritual. Khalil loved the thought of his work bringing comfort to people, of creating something that would be both beautiful and useful, a reminder that art could be a part of everyday life. He imagined someone wrapping their hands around one of his mugs, savoring a moment of peace, finding comfort in the warmth and weight of the clay.

The next piece in his collection was a set of plates, which presented a new set of challenges. Khalil wanted the plates to be functional, but he also wanted them to have a sense of movement, to reflect the themes he had been exploring in his art. He began by shaping the plates with gentle, flowing lines, creating a slightly wavy edge that mimicked the natural curves of leaves or water. Each plate was unique, with a subtle, organic shape that made it feel alive, dynamic. He added textures around the edges, creating a tactile quality that invited people to touch and explore.

When it came to glazing the plates, Khalil chose a different approach, layering colors in a way that created a sense of depth and variation. He used shades of blue, green, and white, blending them to create a look that resembled water rippling across the surface. The effect was subtle yet striking, a reminder of the beauty and movement of nature. Khalil felt a sense of pride as he completed the plates, knowing that he had created pieces that were both functional and meaningful, that brought a sense of art and beauty into the simple act of eating.

As he worked on his collection, Khalil found himself thinking about the idea of connection, about how these pieces would connect him to the people who used them. Each piece carried a part of his story, a piece of his journey, yet it would become part of someone else's life, someone else's story. He loved the thought that his work could bring people together, that it could create moments of connection, of shared experiences.

Khalil decided to showcase his functional collection at a small local market, a place where people gathered to share their art, crafts, and stories. He set up a booth, displaying his bowls, mugs, and plates in an arrangement that invited people to touch, to hold, to interact with the pieces. He wanted people to feel the textures, to see the colors, to experience the art in a tangible way.

As the market opened, people began to visit Khalil's booth, drawn to the earthy colors, the organic shapes, the unique textures. Some people admired the pieces as works of art, commenting on the colors, the forms, the craftsmanship. Others were excited by the idea of using the pieces in their homes, imagining them as part of their daily routines. Khalil loved hearing their reactions, their stories, their connections to his work.

One woman, who was drawn to the bowls, shared how they reminded her of her childhood, of the simple, handmade pottery her family had used. She talked about the comfort of holding something that felt alive, that carried a story. Khalil was moved by her words, realizing that his work had evoked a memory, a connection to her past. He felt a deep sense of fulfillment, knowing that he had created something meaningful, something that had touched her in a personal way.

Another visitor, a young couple, admired the mugs and talked about how they would love to use them in their morning routine, to start their day with something beautiful and handmade. Khalil imagined the mugs becoming a part of their lives, a small but meaningful piece of their story. He realized that his work had the power to bring joy, to create moments of connection, to become a part of people's lives in a way that was both practical and personal.

Throughout the day, Khalil had conversations with people from all walks of life, each one connecting with his work in their own way. He saw how each piece carried its own meaning, its own story, how it could evoke memories, create connections, bring comfort. He felt grateful for the journey that had brought him here, for the opportunity to create work that was both beautiful and functional, that brought art into people's everyday lives.

Chapter 22: Embracing Environmental Sustainability in Art

With his growing commitment to creating pottery that connected with people, Khalil found himself reflecting on another responsibility he felt was vital: environmental sustainability. In his journey as an artist, he had learned that pottery was as much about the earth as it was about expression. Clay, water, and natural glazes were gifts from the planet, and he wanted his work to honor that. As he became more mindful of his materials, he began considering how he could make his art more sustainable, reducing waste and finding ways to give back to the environment that inspired him so deeply.

Khalil started by evaluating his current practices, looking at the materials he used, the energy his kiln required, and the waste generated from his projects. He realized that while clay itself was a natural material, the process of firing it in the kiln consumed significant amounts of energy. He knew there was no perfect solution, but he was determined to explore methods that would lessen his environmental footprint. He researched sustainable practices in pottery, reading about artists who had found creative ways to conserve resources, reduce waste, and even use recycled materials.

His first step toward sustainability was to reduce waste in his studio. He noticed that each project left behind remnants of clay—small, dried-out pieces that would often get swept away and discarded. It felt wasteful, and he wondered if there was a way to recycle this clay. Through his research, he learned that clay could be reclaimed, rehydrated, and reused for new projects. The process was labor-intensive, requiring him to soak the dried pieces in water, then wedge and knead the clay until it was smooth again, but Khalil found it deeply satisfying. By reclaiming the clay, he was giving new life to materials that would otherwise be discarded, turning scraps into fresh clay that he could use in future pieces.

Reclaiming clay soon became a regular part of his routine, and Khalil found himself enjoying the process. Each time he recycled a batch of clay, he felt a sense of gratitude, a connection to the earth and the resources it provided. He began to see his work as part of a cycle, where materials could be transformed and renewed rather than wasted. This approach shifted his perspective, reminding him that art wasn't just about creating something beautiful; it was also about honoring the earth, respecting the materials, and reducing his impact on the environment.

As he continued exploring sustainable practices, Khalil decided to experiment with natural glazes. Traditional ceramic glazes often contained chemicals and heavy metals, which could be harmful to the environment when disposed of improperly. Khalil was intrigued by the idea of creating his own glazes from natural materials, using elements that could be sourced locally and sustainably. He researched natural glaze recipes, learning how to use ashes from burned wood, ground stones, and plant-based ingredients to create colors and textures.

His first experiment was with wood ash glaze, a technique that had been used for centuries in traditional pottery. Khalil collected ash from a friend's fireplace, sifting and grinding it into a fine powder. He mixed the ash with clay slip and applied it to a test piece, curious to see how it would react in the kiln. When the piece was fired, the ash glaze melted into a glossy, organic surface, with subtle variations in color that reflected the natural minerals in the wood ash. The result was rustic and earthy, with a warmth that Khalil hadn't expected. He felt a deep connection to the piece, knowing that it was a creation made entirely from natural materials, sourced locally, and transformed through fire.

Encouraged by the success of his wood ash glaze, Khalil experimented with other natural materials, testing different combinations to achieve unique effects. He used crushed shells to create a soft, pearlescent glaze, and experimented with plant-based stains, which added subtle colors to the clay. Each experiment taught him something new, deepening his appreciation for the earth's resources and the ways they could enhance his work. He loved the unpredictability of natural glazes, the way each piece took on its own character, its own story. Every time he opened the kiln, he felt a sense of anticipation, eager to see how the natural materials had transformed.

As Khalil's commitment to sustainability grew, he began thinking about how he could reduce the energy used in firing his kiln. Firing was an essential part of the pottery process, yet it required a significant amount of energy, especially for larger pieces. Through his research, he learned about low-fire techniques, which required less energy and could still produce beautiful, durable pottery. Khalil began experimenting with low-fire glazes and techniques, adjusting his firing schedule to reduce energy use while maintaining the quality of his work.

He also looked into alternative firing methods, such as pit firing and raku, both of which had lower energy requirements than electric kilns. Pit firing involved burying pottery in a pit filled with combustible materials, like wood and sawdust, and setting it alight. The process was ancient, unpredictable, and filled with surprises, as the smoke and flames left unpredictable patterns on the pottery's surface. Khalil was fascinated by the idea, feeling that it connected him to a tradition of pottery that was both primal and sustainable.

One weekend, he decided to try a pit firing in a nearby open space with the help of a few friends. They dug a shallow pit, filled it with wood, sawdust, and a few natural materials to add color, like salt and leaves. Khalil placed his pieces in the pit, then covered them with more wood and set it alight. They spent the evening around the fire, watching as the flames flickered and danced, occasionally adding more wood to keep the fire going. The process was communal and contemplative, a reminder of the simplicity of creating art in harmony with nature.

When the fire had burned out and the pieces had cooled, Khalil uncovered his pottery, marveling at the unique, smoky patterns left by the fire. Each piece was one-of-a-kind, bearing the marks of the flames, the salt, and the wood ash. Khalil felt a deep satisfaction as he held the pieces, knowing that they had been created with minimal impact on the environment, shaped by fire and earth in a process that was both ancient and sustainable.

As his commitment to environmental sustainability deepened, Khalil began sharing his journey with others. He talked about his experiments with natural glazes, his efforts to reclaim clay, and the challenges of low-fire and pit-firing techniques. He invited other artists to join him in exploring sustainable practices, hoping to inspire a movement toward more eco-friendly pottery. Khalil's friends and fellow artists were intrigued by his methods, and many of them began incorporating similar practices into their own work, experimenting with recycled clay, natural glazes, and alternative firing methods.

One day, Khalil's community center invited him to host a workshop on sustainable pottery, where he could share his practices and teach others about the importance of environmental responsibility in art. Khalil accepted eagerly, excited to spread awareness and inspire others to consider the impact of their materials and processes. During the workshop, he taught participants how to reclaim clay, how to make simple natural glazes from wood ash and crushed shells, and even organized a small pit firing in the center's outdoor space.

The workshop was a success, drawing people of all ages and backgrounds who were interested in learning how to create art in harmony with nature. Khalil was moved by the enthusiasm of the participants, by their openness to learning and their desire to make a positive impact through their art. As he guided them through each step, he felt a sense of fulfillment, knowing that he was contributing to a movement toward sustainability, that he was helping others find ways to honor the earth through their creativity.

After the workshop, Khalil continued to explore new ways to make his art more sustainable. He began sourcing his clay and other materials locally, reducing the environmental impact of transportation. He also started incorporating found materials into his work, like recycled glass, old metal scraps, and even small stones and shells collected from nature. Each piece became a blend of natural and recycled elements, a testament to his commitment to creating art that respected the environment.

Chapter 23: Finding Calm in Art

After delving into sustainability, functionality, and community projects, Khalil felt that his journey as an artist had shifted his focus to a different kind of exploration—a journey inward. He had always found pottery to be a calming process, something that brought him a deep sense of peace and focus. Lately, though, life had become busy, with workshops, markets, and new projects filling his days. While he loved the connections and growth these brought, he began to feel the need for a quieter, more personal form of expression. He wondered if he could intentionally incorporate calmness and mindfulness into his art, creating pieces that not only helped him find peace but also inspired a sense of tranquility in others.

Khalil's first step toward creating art that embodied calmness was to slow down his own process. He had become accustomed to the fast pace of producing pieces for markets, exhibitions, and collaborations, but he knew that if he wanted to infuse peace into his work, he would have to work differently. He began by dedicating a small part of his day to quiet, uninterrupted time in the studio, without a specific goal or deadline. Instead of focusing on a finished product, he allowed himself to focus solely on the act of creation, on the feel of the clay, on the rhythm of his hands shaping it. He found that by letting go of any expectations, he could approach each piece with a sense of openness and curiosity.

As he worked, he noticed how the simple act of centering clay on the wheel required a calm and steady hand. Centering was a process he had done thousands of times, yet he began to see it in a new light. To center the clay, he had to center himself, to bring his mind and body into harmony. He realized that centering clay could be a metaphor for finding balance in life, for grounding oneself amid the noise and busyness of the world. This discovery became a source of inspiration, and he began incorporating this sense of grounding into each piece he created, hoping that the finished work would carry a feeling of calmness and presence.

Khalil also began experimenting with forms that felt serene and balanced. He focused on creating smooth, flowing lines, gentle curves, and rounded shapes that evoked a sense of tranquility. He found that certain shapes, like circles and ovals, brought a natural feeling of calmness, reminding him of the cycles and rhythms of nature. He started creating small bowls and cups with soft, rounded edges, vessels that felt comforting to hold. Each piece was simple, yet he took great care in crafting them, paying attention to every detail, every curve, every line. As he shaped these pieces, he felt a sense of peace wash over him, as if he were creating an oasis of calm in his own life.

Color became another way for Khalil to express calmness in his work. He experimented with soft, muted tones, choosing colors that reminded him of natural elements—the soft blues of a clear sky, the gentle greens of leaves, the warm browns of earth. He avoided bright, intense colors, instead focusing on hues that felt restful, that encouraged a feeling of ease. He carefully layered glazes to create subtle variations in color, adding depth without overwhelming the senses. The finished pieces had a quiet beauty, a simplicity that invited viewers to slow down, to take a moment to breathe and appreciate the details.

As he created these calming pieces, Khalil realized that the process itself was just as important as the finished work. Each piece became a meditation, a way to focus his mind, to connect with the present moment. He found that the slower pace allowed him to be more mindful, to appreciate the feel of the clay, the way it responded to his hands, the sound of the wheel spinning. This sense of mindfulness brought him a deep sense of fulfillment, reminding him of why he had started creating pottery in the first place. It wasn't just about the final piece; it was about the journey, the quiet moments, the peace that came from being fully immersed in the process.

As Khalil's collection of calming pieces grew, he decided to share them with others, hoping that they would bring a sense of peace to those who used them. He organized a small exhibition, calling it "Moments of Calm." The exhibition was designed to be an immersive experience, a space where visitors could slow down, escape the noise of daily life, and connect with a sense of tranquility. He arranged the pieces in a quiet, minimalist setting, with soft lighting and gentle music that complemented the calmness of the pottery.

When the exhibition opened, Khalil was touched by the response. People moved through the space slowly, pausing to admire the pieces, to touch the smooth surfaces, to take in the subtle colors and textures. He noticed how visitors seemed to relax as they spent time in the exhibition, how their expressions softened, how they breathed a little deeper. Some people even closed their eyes, holding one of his pieces in their hands, allowing themselves to feel the weight and texture of the clay, to find comfort in its simplicity. Khalil felt a profound sense of fulfillment, knowing that his work had brought a moment of peace to others, that he had created something that encouraged people to slow down and reconnect with themselves.

One visitor approached Khalil after spending time in the exhibition, sharing how the experience had reminded her of the importance of finding calm in her own life. She spoke about how the simple act of holding one of his cups had brought her a sense of grounding, a reminder to be present, to find beauty in the quiet moments. Khalil was moved by her words, realizing that his art had resonated with her on a personal level. He felt grateful for the opportunity to create work that went beyond aesthetics, that had the power to bring comfort, peace, and reflection.

Another visitor, an artist himself, told Khalil how the exhibition had inspired him to approach his own work with more mindfulness, to focus on the process rather than the product. He shared how he had often felt pressured to create quickly, to produce as much as possible, but that Khalil's work had reminded him of the importance of slowing down, of finding joy in the act of creation. Khalil was deeply touched by the conversation, realizing that his journey into calmness had inspired others to find balance and mindfulness in their own lives.

As the exhibition continued, Khalil spent time observing the visitors, reflecting on his journey and the lessons he had learned. He realized that creating art was not just about expressing himself but also about offering something to others, something that could bring them comfort, peace, and a sense of connection. His work had become a way to share his own experiences, to invite others into the quiet, calming moments that had become so meaningful to him.

The success of "Moments of Calm" inspired Khalil to continue exploring mindfulness in his art. He began creating pieces specifically designed for relaxation, such as small, rounded stones that people could hold in their hands, textured plates that encouraged gentle touch, and even small sculptures that represented serenity and balance. Each piece was crafted with intention, a reminder to slow down, to find calm in the simple act of being present.

Khalil's journey into mindfulness transformed not only his art but also his perspective on life. He began to incorporate the principles of calmness and balance into his daily routine, finding time each day to connect with himself, to center his thoughts, to appreciate the quiet moments. He found that this new approach brought him a deeper sense of fulfillment, a feeling of peace that extended beyond the studio and into every part of his life.

Through his work, Khalil had discovered the power of calmness, the beauty of simplicity, the importance of being present. He realized that art was not just a means of expression but also a way to find peace, to connect with oneself, to create moments of stillness and reflection. His pieces became more than just objects; they became reminders of the calm that was always available, the peace that could be found in the present moment.

Chapter 24: Art as a Form of Healing

Khalil's journey through mindfulness had brought him a new perspective on his art, showing him how creating pottery could be an act of finding inner peace and balance. Yet, as he delved deeper into this quiet side of art, he began to wonder about another layer of its potential impact: could art be a means of healing, not only for himself but for others? He thought back on his own experiences, on how working with clay had helped him through moments of doubt, anxiety, and self-discovery. Art had been a path to resilience, a way to transform difficult emotions into something beautiful. Khalil began to see that art could offer a form of healing, a process through which pain could find expression and even transformation.

This idea grew stronger when Khalil met a young woman named Zara, who visited his studio one day. Zara had recently experienced a deep personal loss, and a friend had suggested pottery as a therapeutic outlet. When she entered the studio, Khalil noticed her gentle yet guarded demeanor. She looked around with cautious interest, as though unsure of what to expect. He greeted her warmly, inviting her to sit by the wheel, to feel the clay, to connect with its texture and potential. At first, she hesitated, her hands hovering uncertainly over the material, but with Khalil's gentle encouragement, she began shaping the clay, letting her fingers sink into its softness.

As she worked, Khalil saw a transformation. Zara seemed to become absorbed in the act of creating, her initial hesitancy giving way to a quiet focus. The clay offered her a release, a way to channel her emotions without words. It wasn't about creating something perfect; it was about allowing herself to feel, to let her hands speak what her heart couldn't. Khalil guided her through the process, reminding her to take her time, to focus on the feel of the clay, to let her emotions flow through her hands. As he watched her work, he realized that pottery could be more than a personal journey. It could be a form of healing, a way to help others find peace, strength, and expression.

Inspired by his experience with Zara, Khalil decided to explore the idea of art therapy more deeply. He began reading about the ways in which creative expression could be a tool for emotional healing, learning about art therapists who used various mediums to help people process grief, trauma, and stress. The more he learned, the more he felt a desire to create a space where others could experience the healing power of art. He wanted his studio to be a sanctuary, a place where people could come to release their burdens, to transform pain into beauty, to find solace in the act of creating.

Khalil reached out to a few local counselors and therapists, sharing his vision of using pottery as a therapeutic practice. Many of them were intrigued, seeing the potential for clay to help their clients connect with emotions that might be difficult to express in words. Together, they developed a program called "Hands and Heart," a series of workshops designed to use pottery as a form of healing. The program would invite people to experience the therapeutic aspects of working with clay, to explore the connection between their hands and their emotions, to find expression through the art of pottery.

The first "Hands and Heart" workshop was attended by a small, intimate group of participants, each with their own story, their own reasons for seeking healing through art. Some had experienced loss, others were dealing with anxiety, and a few simply wanted to explore a new way of connecting with themselves. Khalil welcomed them warmly, explaining that this workshop was not about creating a perfect piece of pottery but about using the clay as a way to process emotions, to connect with one's inner self. He encouraged them to approach the clay with openness, to allow themselves to feel without judgment, to let their hands shape what their hearts held.

As the participants began working, Khalil moved among them, offering quiet guidance, gentle words of encouragement. He noticed how each person approached the clay differently, some with tentative hands, others with a sense of urgency. One man, who had recently lost a loved one, worked in silence, his hands moving steadily as he shaped a simple bowl. Khalil saw the tension in his face, the weight of his grief, and he understood that the bowl he was creating was more than just an object—it was a vessel for his sorrow, a way to hold and honor his pain.

Another participant, a young woman dealing with stress and anxiety, created a series of small, intricate pieces, each one reflecting her need for control and order. Khalil could see how she poured herself into the details, using the act of creation to find a sense of stability and focus. He encouraged her to let go of perfection, to allow herself to make mistakes, to see beauty in the imperfect. As she loosened her grip on the clay, her pieces began to take on a more organic, flowing quality, reflecting a sense of freedom she hadn't expected to find.

Throughout the workshop, Khalil felt a profound sense of fulfillment. He saw how each person found their own path to healing through the clay, how the act of creating allowed them to release emotions they had been holding inside. He realized that his role was not to teach them how to create pottery but to create a space where they could heal, where they could find peace, where they could transform their pain into something tangible. The workshop became a place of quiet strength, a reminder that healing was a journey, one that could be supported and shared through the act of creation.

As "Hands and Heart" grew, more people from the community joined the workshops, each bringing their own stories, their own reasons for seeking healing. Khalil continued to witness the transformative power of art, the way it allowed people to connect with their emotions, to process grief, to find comfort in the act of creating. He saw how pottery became a form of expression, a language through which people could communicate their inner worlds. Each piece they created, whether a bowl, a vase, or an abstract shape, carried a piece of their journey, a reflection of their resilience, their hope, their strength.

One participant, an elderly woman who had been quietly shaping a series of small figures, approached Khalil after a workshop, her eyes filled with gratitude. She shared how the process had helped her come to terms with her husband's passing, how each figure she shaped felt like a way to honor his memory. She told Khalil that for the first time since his death, she had felt a sense of peace, a feeling that he was still with her in some way. Khalil was deeply moved by her words, understanding that the healing she had found was a testament to the power of art, a reminder of why he had started this journey.

Through these experiences, Khalil learned that art was not just a means of self-expression; it was a path to healing, a way to connect with oneself, to find strength in times of darkness. He saw how pottery could be a form of therapy, a way to hold space for emotions, to allow them to be seen, felt, and transformed. His studio had become a sanctuary, a place where people could come to heal, to find comfort, to reconnect with themselves.

As he reflected on this journey, Khalil felt a profound sense of gratitude. He was grateful for the clay, for its ability to hold and reflect emotions, for its resilience and strength. He was grateful for the people who had come to his studio, who had trusted him with their stories, who had allowed him to witness their healing. He felt humbled by their courage, by the way they had embraced the clay as a means of healing, by the strength they had found through the act of creation.

Khalil's journey into healing through art had transformed not only his perspective on pottery but also his understanding of what it meant to be an artist. He realized that his work was not just about creating beautiful pieces but about creating spaces for healing, for connection, for resilience. His studio had become a place where people could come to find peace, to release their burdens, to transform their pain into something meaningful.

Khalil's "Hands and Heart" workshops continued to grow, reaching more people, offering a space where they could find peace, strength, and connection. Through this journey, he learned that art could be a bridge, a way to connect with others, to offer comfort, to hold space for emotions that were often too heavy to bear alone. His work had become a gift, a way to give back, to support others, to honor the beauty and resilience of the human spirit.

Chapter 25: Embracing Legacy and the Journey Ahead

As Khalil looked around his studio, he felt a mixture of gratitude and wonder at the journey that had brought him to this point. The walls were lined with pieces from every chapter of his life: the early, simple bowls that first sparked his interest, the experimental forms that stretched his imagination, the culturally inspired symbols, and the functional yet beautiful pottery designed to bring calm into people's lives. Every piece told a story, each one a marker of growth, struggle, and discovery. And now, standing in this studio surrounded by a lifetime of creativity, Khalil felt a sense of peace, as if he had finally come to understand the full purpose of his journey.

Over the past few months, Khalil had been thinking deeply about his legacy. It wasn't just about the art he created, but about the impact he left behind—the people he had taught, the community projects he had led, the workshops that had touched so many lives. Art had been his means of connecting with others, of exploring life's many questions, of finding meaning in both joy and sorrow. He realized that his legacy was not only about his pottery but about the way he had shared his passion, the way he had invited others to explore their own creativity, to find healing, comfort, and inspiration in art.

One day, as he pondered these thoughts, he received a visit from a former student named Aminah. She had been part of his early workshops and had continued her journey in pottery, eventually becoming an artist in her own right. Aminah had come to share some exciting news—she was planning to open her own studio, inspired by Khalil's teachings and her own love for pottery. She expressed her gratitude to Khalil, explaining how his encouragement and guidance had given her the confidence to pursue her dreams.

Khalil was deeply moved by her words. Aminah's journey reminded him of the power of mentorship, of the impact that teaching could have on another person's life. He realized that this was part of his legacy as well, that the knowledge and inspiration he had shared with others would continue to grow and evolve, carried forward by those who had found their own paths through art. Seeing Aminah's joy and confidence, he felt a deep sense of pride, knowing that his work had contributed to her journey.

This visit sparked an idea in Khalil. He wanted to create something lasting, something that would continue to inspire future generations of artists. He decided to establish a foundation, one that would support young, aspiring artists who didn't have the resources to pursue their dreams. The foundation would provide scholarships, mentorship, and access to a studio, offering a space where young artists could explore their creativity, learn from experienced potters, and find their own voices.

Setting up the foundation was a new experience for Khalil. It required careful planning, collaboration, and support from others who shared his vision. He reached out to friends, fellow artists, and community leaders, inviting them to join him in building this legacy. The response was overwhelmingly positive, and soon, he had a team of people working together to bring his vision to life. They secured a space in the heart of the community, a studio that would be open to anyone with a passion for art, regardless of their background or experience.

The foundation was named "The Clay Path," a tribute to the journey of discovery that art could offer. Khalil envisioned it as a place where people of all ages could come to explore pottery, to learn, to connect, and to heal. He wanted it to be more than just a studio; he wanted it to be a space where people could find purpose, meaning, and joy in the act of creation. Through The Clay Path, Khalil hoped to inspire others to follow their own paths, to see art as a journey of growth and self-discovery.

As The Clay Path began its work, Khalil found himself deeply involved in mentoring young artists. He spent hours in the studio, guiding them through the basics, encouraging them to experiment, and helping them find their own styles. Each young artist brought their own unique perspective, their own dreams and challenges, and Khalil felt a deep sense of fulfillment in supporting them. He saw in their eyes the same excitement he had felt when he first discovered pottery, the same curiosity and passion. It reminded him of the beauty of beginnings, of the endless possibilities that lay before each of them.

One of the young artists, a teenager named Jamal, showed a natural talent for pottery but struggled with self-doubt. He often hesitated to finish his pieces, fearing they wouldn't be good enough. Khalil recognized this hesitation, remembering his own struggles with insecurity. He took Jamal under his wing, encouraging him to embrace imperfection, to see each piece as a step forward rather than a final product. Khalil taught him to focus on the process, to find joy in each stage of creation. Over time, he saw Jamal's confidence grow, his hands becoming steadier, his heart more open to his own potential.

Another student, a young woman named Leila, had a powerful story of resilience. She had faced many challenges in her life and had turned to art as a way to heal. Pottery became her sanctuary, a place where she could express her emotions and find peace. Khalil watched as she poured her heart into her work, creating pieces that held a quiet strength, a beauty born from perseverance. He admired her courage, her dedication, and he felt honored to be part of her journey, to offer her a space where she could find solace and strength.

Through his work with these young artists, Khalil saw the impact of The Clay Path. He realized that this was his legacy—a place where people could find inspiration, healing, and connection, a place that would continue to nurture creativity long after he was gone. His heart swelled with gratitude for the journey that had led him here, for the people who had supported him, for the community that had embraced his vision.

As The Clay Path continued to grow, Khalil also began reflecting on his own journey, on the lessons he had learned, the challenges he had overcome, and the beauty he had found in art. He felt a sense of completion, a feeling that he had come full circle. He no longer felt the need to prove himself, to push boundaries, or to create for the sake of recognition. He had found peace in his work, a quiet fulfillment that came from knowing he had made a difference, that he had used his art to bring beauty, comfort, and inspiration to others.

One evening, as he sat in his studio, Khalil picked up a piece of clay and began shaping it without any particular purpose. His hands moved instinctively, guided by years of experience, by a lifetime of working with this material. The clay felt familiar, comforting, like an old friend. He shaped it into a simple bowl, feeling a sense of calm as he worked. He realized that this moment, this quiet, unhurried act of creation, was a reflection of his journey—a reminder that art was not just about the finished piece but about the process, the connection, the experience of being fully present.

As he completed the bowl, he felt a sense of gratitude for everything that had brought him here, for the moments of doubt and triumph, for the people who had touched his life, for the lessons he had learned. He knew that his journey would continue, that there were still stories to tell, pieces to create, and lives to touch. But he also felt a deep peace, a belief that he had fulfilled his purpose, that he had created a legacy that would live on.

Khalil's journey as an artist had been a path of discovery, of growth, of connection. He had found himself in the art of pottery, had healed through the act of creation, and had shared his passion with others. His legacy was not just in the pieces he had created but in the lives he had touched, in the inspiration he had given to others, in the foundation he had built. The Clay Path would continue his work, offering a place for future generations to explore, to create, to find their own paths.

Don't miss out!

Visit the website below and you can sign up to receive emails whenever Eli Turner publishes a new book. There's no charge and no obligation.

https://books2read.com/r/B-A-AKLVC-VROIF

BOOKS 2 READ

Connecting independent readers to independent writers.

Did you love *Khalil's Clay Creations*? Then you should read *Kai's Quest for Harmony*[1] by Sylvia Mooncrest!

Kai's Quest for Harmony is a journey into the heart of nature and beyond, where young Kai embarks on a musical adventure to gather the sounds of the world. From mountains and forests to oceans and stars, Kai discovers the voices of nature and the beauty of diversity. Along the way, he learns valuable lessons about unity, connection, and kindness. Filled with heartwarming encounters, Kai's journey reminds readers that the world is full of unique voices, each contributing to the melody of life. Perfect for inspiring children ages 5-10 to appreciate harmony in all its forms.

---

1. https://books2read.com/u/49qJAW
2. https://books2read.com/u/49qJAW

About the Publisher

Whimsy Tales Press is a creative powerhouse devoted to publishing exceptional children's books that spark joy, imagination, and lifelong learning. With a mission to inspire young minds, the company crafts stories that celebrate diversity, kindness, and the magic of discovery. Whimsy Tales Press collaborates with passionate authors and illustrators to bring captivating characters and enchanting worlds to life. From heartwarming bedtime tales to empowering adventures, every book is designed to entertain while fostering empathy and curiosity. Committed to excellence and inclusivity, Whimsy Tales Press ensures that each story leaves a lasting impression, encouraging children to dream big and believe in endless possibilities.

Milton Keynes UK
Ingram Content Group UK Ltd.
UKHW020914291124
451807UK00013B/913

9 798227 262233